MARGARET L.
CARTER

Love Unleashed

Ellora's Cave
Romantica Publishing

What the critics are saying...

ꕥ

4 Hearts "Margaret Carter has written a nicely crafted tale of magic, redemption and love. The dream sequences will leave you panting and waiting for more. I look forward to reading more books by this talented author." ~ *The Romance Studio*

An Ellora's Cave Romantica Publication

www.ellorascave.com

Love Unleashed

ISBN 9781419960086

Edited by Pamela Campbell.
Photography and cover art by Les Byerley.

This book printed in the U.S.A. by Jasmine-Jade Enterprises, LLC.

Electronic book publication February 2008
Trade paperback publication September 2009

LOVE UNLEASHED

Acknowledgements

With thanks to Ilene Caroom, who provided information on legal procedures. Any errors are my own.

Trademarks Acknowledgement

ல

The author acknowledges the trademarked status and trademark owners of the following wordmarks mentioned in this work of fiction:

Chanel: Chanel Inc. Corporation

Gentle Leader: Ameri-Pet Inc. Corporation

Lexus: Toyota Jidosha Kabushiki Kaisha Corporation

SPCA: SPCA International Inc.

Chapter One

ꟓ

A chill slithered down Stefan's spine in spite of the sun that shone through the high, narrow windows. *The minute Diana invited me here in the middle of the week, I should have run the other way.* Candles in sconces on the walls shed their glow over the labyrinth painted onto the polished floor of the below-ground chamber. Noticing the rope of twisted crimson cords she held, he had a feeling he also should have insisted on finishing the conversation upstairs in the living room. Although dressed in cargo shorts and a casual blouse instead of her ceremonial robes, the tall blonde looked imposing enough to intimidate a novice. Which he wasn't, of course.

Still, he knew he'd been wise to keep Diana at a coolly friendly distance, treating her as a colleague, not a potential lover. And not because she had a few years on him. With her firm, high breasts and ice-queen beauty, she looked so youthful for her mid-forties that he suspected her of enhancing her charms with magic.

He faced her with his arms folded, striking a deliberately arrogant posture. "What happened to 'Do what thou wilt'?"

"What happened to the ethics of not violating the will of another? I trusted you, Stefan." She untied one of the nine knots in the rope. A whisper of power ghosted across the bare skin of his forearms.

So that's what this is all about. He stifled a sigh. "I didn't do anything against Tanith's true will."

"My daughter is too young to know her true will, especially when she's dealing with an adept like you."

"Thanks for the compliment. She isn't a kid, though. She's over twenty-one. I think she can make her own choices." He mentally kicked himself for getting involved with the daughter of his coven's priestess, even briefly. Not that he made a habit of more than brief relationships with any woman. He hadn't kept his past liaisons a secret from Tanith, so what did either she or her mother have to complain about?

"What you did to her—how do I know choice had anything to do with it?" Diana's hands shook as she untied the second knot. The late afternoon sunlight momentarily dimmed as if obscured by a thundercloud.

Stefan brushed aside the uneasiness that stirred in him. Indignation replaced his mild annoyance. "I have never used magic to lure a woman into bed. Never." He tamped down the anger and shrugged. "A little aura of attractiveness to get things going, at most. I didn't need that with Tanith."

If human eyes could flash, Diana's would be shooting sparks. "You're the priest of her coven. She looked up to you. Of course you had no trouble seducing her." She moved on to the third knot. Shadows deepened in the corners of the room.

Illusion. She's trying to spook me. "Seducing? You sound like a Victorian novel. She needed comfort and I happened to be around. It was mutual." He sighed aloud this time, spreading his hands in a conciliatory gesture. "What are you so worked up about anyway? It's not like she was a virgin."

The girl had at least one prior relationship that Stefan knew of. In fact, she'd been going with another man in their circle, one closer to her own age. After she'd had a fight with him, she had accepted Stefan's shoulder to cry on. When comfort had heated to passion, he hadn't hesitated. He and Tanith had enjoyed two months together. At least, he'd enjoyed it, he reflected with a reminiscent smile. He hadn't noticed any indication that she'd felt otherwise.

Diana's face momentarily contorted with rage. Unclenching her teeth, she smoothed over her expression, though her fingers kept untwisting the cords. "Yes, and thanks to you, Rob won't have anything to do with her. He was good for her and they would have gotten back together if you hadn't interfered."

"Damn it, I'm not responsible for Tanith's love life. We had a casual thing. That's perfectly legitimate in the philosophy this coven follows or have you switched the rules and I missed the memo?"

"It's legitimate between equals. Tanith is twenty-four. You're thirty-five and far more experienced. She thought you meant something by it. I could have told her different but of course she wouldn't listen to her mother. Even when her mother is also her priestess." By now Diana had worked her way up to the sixth knot.

"I never made any kind of commitment. I didn't lead her astray with false vows like a helpless maiden in a melodrama. Crawling Chaos, next you'll try to force me to marry her." He glanced up at the patch of daylight visible through the nearest window. The longer this conversation went on, the more trapped he felt. He hoped Diana would finish her tirade soon so he could escape.

"That's the last thing I'd want to foist on her. But I'm not about to let you get away with this." She finished unbinding the seventh knot. Her magic blew past him like a gust of wind.

He ignored it and smirked at her. "Breach of promise lawsuits are out of style too."

The darkening of Diana's aura warned him that mocking her was a mistake. "My daughter's been crying her eyes out over you for the past week. Granted, I think she's acting like an idiot. You aren't worth it. You don't know how to care about anybody. I believe the only creature you've loved in the past twenty years was that scruffy cat of yours that died a few months ago."

He winced inwardly but kept his face carefully neutral. Damned if he'd let Diana guess she'd succeeded in wounding him. One reason he'd stopped hanging out with Tanith was the well-meaning way she kept nagging him to find another cat. She insisted he needed a new pet in order to "get over" Caesar's death. "Animals don't lie to you. They don't make unreasonable demands. They seldom let you down and they're much more relaxing company than people."

"Just the kind of thing I'd expect you to say." The chill in her voice seared him like dry ice. "I've watched you jump from one woman to the next like a dog chasing bitches in heat. For a powerful magus, you have a worse case of arrested development than any other man I've ever met. But it wasn't any of my business until now." The eighth knot came loose.

"I don't see how it's your business now, either. It's between me and your daughter. Why don't you bring her down here and let her speak for herself?"

"I wouldn't force her to set foot in the same room with you. You've done enough to her already." Power shimmered around her and an aroma like wood smoke scorched the air. "Did you know she's pregnant?"

"What? Wait a minute! Surely you don't think it's mine?" Impossible, he'd been much too careful.

Diana snorted. "Don't be ridiculous. I know it's Rob's. But it's his belief that matters. His doubts make things that much worse between him and Tanith."

Stefan fingered the silver amulet, engraved with a pentacle, that he'd worn since his old mentor had presented it to him upon his initiation. It served as a reservoir for his magic and he felt the need for its occult energy now. "Look, Diana, I'm sorry she misunderstood my intentions. She'll get over it. Just one of those things everybody goes through sooner or later." He meant that statement sincerely enough. He'd never wanted to make Tanith miserable. He liked her. He just couldn't fathom why Diana had to turn the situation into such a big deal. *Women!*

"So you don't intend to apologize?"

"For what? Like I said—she's a big girl. What are you planning to do about it? Put a curse on me?" His smile faded as the mist of power around her coalesced into a thundercloud. *Loki and Hermes help me! That's exactly what she's going to do!*

"You're going to pay. You will become what you are. You will stay in that form until you learn to care, until you become truly human. So mote it be." She released the ninth knot then tied the ends of the rope together into a circle. Arcane syllables poured from her mouth.

Powers of Chaos, she had a spell stored in it! Cramps seized his arms and legs. His stomach clenched in agony. His whole body doubled over in painful contortions, while an itch like a thousand fire ants swarmed over his skin. He collapsed onto hands and knees in the middle of the circle. Blinded by a dark cloud that churned before his eyes, he struggled for breath against a weight that crushed his chest. In the midst of the torment, he was dimly aware of his clothes ripping and falling off. *Gods, I had no idea she was this powerful!* Naked, he clutched the silver disk hanging around his neck. Focusing on it, he groped for the dissipating threads of his own power. Through the confusion howling inside his skull, he realized his only hope was to shape the spell Diana was casting on him.

As the magic ensnared him, he grasped and twisted it. He sensed he had little time left before she completed the curse. *What is she trying to do?* The next moment, he knew. He felt his nails turn to claws, his teeth and ears lengthen, fur sprout on his skin and something rip from the base of his spine in a final burst of pain. He was becoming a beast, a literal one. *Become what you are,* she'd commanded. He diverted as much of her power as he could through the channels of his own will. *Let me keep my humanity – some of it at least. Don't let me lose myself. And don't let her hold me captive. Shield me from her magic. Guide me to a place of refuge.* Darkness thickened around him.

When his vision cleared a second later, colors had faded to grays and pastels. Odors, on the other hand, had sharpened to stinging intensity. With no effort he recognized the bayberry fragrance of the candles, the dust under the altar, Diana's

Chanel perfume, the musky aroma of her flesh and the charred scent of her anger. He glanced down and saw his arms transmuted to legs covered with white hair. He opened his jaws to scream and the sound came out as a howl.

Panic flooded him. Diana's invisible web entangled his limbs. With a surge of terror, he shredded the strands of power and dashed out through the adjoining room to the stairs. Her shriek of rage pursued him. He felt a bolt of magic strike him and dissolve on contact. *Good, the shielding worked,* he thought in the small corner of his brain that remained rational.

Mindlessly barking, he charged up the steps to the kitchen, redolent of a spicy bean soup simmering on the stove. The tiny human compartment of his mind noted an open window with an exposed screen. Diana's footsteps clattered up the basement stairs after him, while Tanith's scurried down from the second floor. As she ran into the kitchen, Stefan heard her yell, "Mother, what have you done now?" He ignored her, pouring all his strength into a leap onto the edge of the sink. His momentum propelled him into the window and knocked the screen out.

He hit the ground with his front legs, rolled onto his side and sprang to his feet. The noise of his own barking made his ears hurt but he couldn't stop. Fear and the urgency of escape consumed him. Although no longer able to form coherent thoughts, he sensed how important it was to evade the woman who chased him, bristling with magic. He rushed toward the back fence—solid redwood, four feet high. He jumped, snagged his front paws on the top and braced his rear paws on the crossbar halfway up. He scrambled over, dropped onto the ground on the other side and stretched his legs to their top speed.

The shore cut off his escape behind the fence. He circled around the side yard of Diana's waterfront lot and ran parallel to the street. He needed a refuge, somewhere to hide or someone to shelter him. That place or person called to him, though he had no idea what or who it might be. It drew him like an irresistible scent. The afternoon heat smothered him like the inside of an oven but he didn't dare slow down. Panting, his lungs aching and his heart pounding, he raced toward that call.

* * * * *

Funny, how one simple gesture toward seizing control of her life could make her whole perspective on the world shift. The sunny August afternoon looked especially cheerful to Vicki, now that she had herself and her property safely cleared out of her significant other's townhouse. No, ex-significant other, if there was such a term. *Whatever – good riddance.* She glanced at her brother Nick, in the driver's seat of the SUV whose interior was half filled with her assorted boxes. "Thanks again for taking time off work to help me. It would've taken me a couple of trips to haul this stuff in my car and I'm afraid I might've lost my nerve by the second go-round." She'd spent so much time at Phil's place over the past two years that she'd piled up a surprisingly large heap of clothes and other paraphernalia there.

"The General Assembly's not in session. They can spare me for one afternoon." Nick, a lawyer, worked downtown on State Circle as a legislative drafter for the state. "You should've known I'd jump at the chance to get you away from that jerk before you changed your mind."

"No fear of that. I should have known from the beginning that a guy who kept a gun instead of a dog for protection wasn't my type." She suppressed a sigh, with doubts and self-reproach buzzing in her head like a hive of wasps. How could she have misjudged Phil so completely and wasted so much of her life on him? "The first real clue was when he started badgering me to sell my house and move in with him full-time and he wouldn't take no for an answer."

"For a while there I was afraid you might do it."

"No way!" The house in Eastport, just a mile from her workplace, had belonged to their parents. When their widowed mother had died, Vicki had bought Nick's half and continued to live there. Without that financial break, she would have had trouble surviving in this area on her salary. "But Phil just thought I was being silly. Sentimental, he said. Then the last straw was that shouting match the other day while my car was in the shop." Today, her first free day since that ridiculous fight, she'd cleared out.

"Over the guy who works at the vet's office with you?" Nick grinned and shook his head. "Don't get me wrong, he seems nice but he's not your type at all. Too young, for one thing."

Vicki swatted him on the arm. "Yeah, like I'm over the hill at twenty-nine."

"Anyway, old Phil must be delusional, thinking you'd cheat on him. You're the faithful type."

"Thanks, you make me sound like the family dog." She mentally sighed again. Probably that loyal streak was what had made her stick with Phil long after she started having doubts. Or was it that she just had no judgment about men?

Nick slowed the car on the curve just before the strip mall where she worked as a veterinary technician. "Are you sure you're doing the right thing, leaving Phil this way, without telling him in advance? He doesn't seem like the type to accept that too calmly."

"Yeah, I know I'm taking the coward's way out but I couldn't face another argument. I left a note with the spare key he gave me. He'll get the idea."

"What if he comes after you?"

"To do what? He may be a jerk, like you said, but he isn't dangerous."

"I'm not so sure about that. He never paid much attention to anything you said. How do you know he'll accept that you really mean it about breaking up?"

"He'll believe I'm serious when he sees I've moved my stuff out, that's what. Don't worry about it." Sometimes she appreciated big-brother protectiveness but other times it felt more constricting than comforting. Since their mother's death, Nick tended to treat Vicki as if the age gap between them was more than the actual four years. He looked more like a twin than her elder, with his chestnut hair and neatly trimmed beard still free of gray. She had hair of the same color, except for her auburn highlights, and they both had blue eyes.

"Maybe you should get another dog, just in case."

"To protect me from the big bad beltway bandit?" she said, referring to Phil's job with a defense contracting firm in Washington. She laughed at the idea of any danger from uptight, supercivilized Phil Garrett. He favored sarcasm rather than violence as a weapon.

"Trixie has been dead almost a year. You need a dog around the house. There are other dangers for a woman on her own, you know."

"Come on, I don't live in the rough part of town or anything like that." She brushed aside the wistful memory of the old Border collie she'd inherited from their folks along with the house.

"Annapolis isn't that big a town. The rough part is only a couple of miles from the safe part."

"Mom and Dad lived in that house for most of their lives and never had any trouble." She glanced ahead at the vet's storefront office, where they were going to pick up her paycheck before driving back to her home to unload the SUV. "Maybe you're right about a new pet, though. Symbolic fresh start, first day of the rest of my life and all that." If she didn't fall in instant love with a puppy at the SPCA, the doctors she worked for could steer her toward a local breeder. Or maybe she should get a cat, which would be less trouble. Phil claimed to be allergic, so she hadn't been able to consider a kitten before now. There were lots of things she could do now that she didn't have to worry about his quirks.

Just as Nick turned into the parking lot, a huge brown and white blur hurtled toward Vicki's window. She let out a screech. Nick slammed on the brakes and the thing rammed into the passenger door.

Vicki jumped out, her heart hammering, and fell to her knees beside the animal. It lay on its side, apparently stunned. Nick hurried around the car to join her. "Good grief, a kamikaze dog," he said.

The creature was the biggest Saint Bernard she'd ever seen. When she touched its head, the chocolate-brown eyes flickered open for a second. "We have to get him into the office right away."

"I'm not about to carry him across the parking lot. Help me lift him into the car." After pulling out of the path of traffic, Nick shifted boxes to clear a space in the back of the SUV. Meanwhile, Vicki felt over the dog's legs, hips and rib cage.

"I don't think anything's broken." She cradled the animal's head and neck, while her brother handled the bulk of the weight. Together, they hefted the half-conscious dog into the vehicle.

"See, it's an omen," Nick said. "Practically the minute I said you needed a pet, a dog came along and threw himself at you."

"Well, I can't keep this one. I'm sure he belongs to somebody. He's wearing something around his neck."

Nick drove the car up to the vet's office, luckily finding a parking space only two slots from the door. Vicki ran inside to ask for help. Fred, a vet tech in his early twenties with curly hair and one gold earring, was covering the front desk. Stressful though the argument had been at the time, she almost giggled at the memory of Phil's accusation when he'd picked her up after work the other day and spotted her chatting with Fred. As Nick had implied, her young coworker was a nice enough guy but one of the last people she'd consider fooling around with. He glanced up when the bell above the door rang. "Hi. You're here for your check, right?"

"Yeah but I also brought a patient. A dog ran into Nick's car. Could you help us bring him in?"

On the way out, Fred asked, "Don't you mean the car ran into the dog?"

"Not exactly."

Fred and Nick lugged the animal inside. The only other patient in the waiting room was a caged cat, who hissed at the sight of the dog. When they laid him on the floor, he opened his eyes, started panting and gave a feeble thump of his tail. Vicki knelt down and stroked his head. His tongue flicked out to brush her hand. "I didn't want to take the time to drive him all the way across town to the emergency vet. Do you think one of the docs can fit him in?"

"I'll check." Fred went into the back room and returned almost immediately with the reply that Dr. Brodie, the senior partner, had a few minutes free. "Big one, isn't he?" he said, eying the dog. "Might as well try to weigh him."

When they started to lift the dog, he struggled to his feet, still panting. With Vicki's fingers twined in his neck fur, he wobbled over to the flatbed scale. He stood quietly while they waited for the digital readout to appear. Fred whistled. "Almost a hundred and ninety pounds. You're a big one, aren't you?"

While Nick waited out front, the two of them managed to get the dog to stagger into the examining room under his own power. Fred coaxed him onto the table then operated the hydraulic lift to raise it to a comfortable level for the examiner. The dog's droopy eyes shifted to follow Vicki's every move. She fondled the black velvet of his ears and rubbed the back of his neck. "What in the world is this?" Her probing revealed a chain of fine silver links. When she worked it over his head, it turned out to be a necklace with a disk about the size of an old-fashioned silver dollar, embossed with a five-pointed star, dangling from it.

Fred stared at the thing when she held it up. "Why would anybody put jewelry on an animal?"

"I have no idea. And no collar, just this." The dog turned his head to follow the movement of her hand and whined as if he wanted his ornament back. "Sorry, it looks too valuable. I'd better hang on to it for you."

He growled when Fred lifted his tail to insert the thermometer. "Easy, boy," Vicki said. "I can't blame you but you have to put up with it." With a heavy sigh, the animal let his head sag onto the table.

Dr. Brodie walked in a minute later. He had shaggy gray hair and a matching mustache that made him look to Vicki like a sheepdog wearing glasses. After glancing at the chart where Fred had recorded the vital statistics, he said, "He's a little overheated but that's more likely from running, not a fever. So what happened, exactly?"

"Close encounter with my brother's SUV." She described the collision.

"He's probably lost, running around in a panic." Dr. Brodie ran his hands over the animal's body. Pressure on the abdomen provoked a muffled yelp but no resistance. "Good boy. Nothing broken and no sign of internal injuries. He wasn't wearing a collar?"

"No, just this." She held up the necklace.

"Strange." Murmuring to himself, the doctor finished the examination with a check of eyes, ears and mouth. "He's in perfect health, aside from a few bruises and the aftereffects of ramming the car with his head. Pupils normally reactive, so I don't think there's much damage. An intact male—show quality if I'm any judge. His coat is in beautiful condition except for dirt from the parking lot. Classic markings—black mask, white tail tip and paws. Somebody's bound to be looking for this big guy. We'll check for a microchip."

Fred brought in the handheld reader and skimmed over the dog's shoulder blades. "Nothing there." He tried other locations, keeping an eye on the LED display. "Nope, nada."

"Why would anybody hang an expensive piece of jewelry on a dog and not bother attaching an ID?" The doctor shook his head. "Some people don't deserve pets."

"I guess I'd better place an ad," Vicki said. "Like you said, somebody must be missing him."

"Normally I'd suggest you drop him at the animal shelter before they close but he should be watched tonight in case of concussion. Maybe you should take him to the twenty-four hour animal hospital. With luck, you might be able to get the owner to reimburse you."

The dog lifted his head, gazed at her and whimpered. "Look at that, you'd think he understood. Don't worry, I'm not about to desert you, big fella. You can stay at my place tonight." She tucked the silver necklace into her purse for safekeeping.

"We'll give you some pain pills just in case he shows signs of discomfort," the doctor said. "I know I can trust you not to use them if there's any doubt about brain damage. What are you going to call him?"

She smiled at the dog, which licked her hand. "Well, certainly not Cujo or Beethoven."

"Too obvious. So is Barney. How about Barry, after the famous Swiss rescue dog?"

"No, I don't think I'll call him anything," she decided. "That would just confuse him. He's got to have a name already." Since he was still panting, she asked for a bowl of water. When Fred delivered it, the dog gulped it down with sloppy eagerness, splashing a puddle onto the linoleum.

In the waiting room she paid for the painkillers, silently grateful to Dr. Brodie for waiving the exam fee and chose a leash and choke collar from the display next to the bags and cans of premium food.

Ringing up her purchases, Fred said, "Shouldn't you get a Gentle Leader? If he pulls on a regular collar, you'll never be able to hold him."

"Yeah, I guess so. I'll get one of those instead." She returned the choke chain to the rack. "And food." She mentally cringed at the price of the dry kibble she picked out. Even with her mortgage only half the market value of the house, she didn't have much wiggle room in her budget for expensive pet food. *So it's a good thing I'm not keeping him for long, isn't it?*

The dog licked her hand again as she looped the Gentle Leader over his muzzle and fastened the collar portion. "He likes you," Nick said, taking her bag of supplies.

"I'll try not to be too flattered," she said, "since I've never met a Saint Bernard that didn't like everybody." She waved goodbye to Fred and coaxed the dog toward the exit.

"So if you don't find the owner, are you going to keep him?" her brother asked.

"You've got to be kidding. When I said I might get another pet, I meant a cute little puppy, not a horse with fur." She hoped neither Nick nor the dog could tell how tempting the idea sounded. "I'm not keeping you, dog. Definitely not. Not a chance. Stop looking at me that way."

He climbed docilely into the car and lay on his side. Vicki kept a loose grasp of the leash in case his mood changed when the engine started. He still breathed heavily but not as rapidly or noisily as before, so she didn't worry too much about his condition. With the August heat, some panting was to be expected. He stayed calm while Nick drove her to the nearby bank to deposit her paycheck, then home. Her house sat on a side street in an older residential area halfway between downtown Annapolis and Forest Drive, the four-lane road that marked the city-county line.

In her front yard, she paused to pat the giant inflatable crab next to the porch steps. "Can you believe it—Phil kept bugging me to get rid of this?"

Nick shook his head in mock horror. "Dump the crab? Outrageous."

"I told him it gave the place character." Each fall she replaced it with a giant inflatable pumpkin and in winter she set up a snowman of similar material. The dog shied away from the fire-engine-red mammoth crustacean with a tentative flick of his tail. "Don't worry, big guy, it's harmless. Phil just has no sense of fun."

She guided the dog into the fenced backyard. His gait didn't look unsteady anymore. Bumping into the car must not have done him any permanent harm. Not wanting to release him until she felt more confident that he wouldn't try to escape at the first opportunity, she held on to the lead and waited. He paced to the end of the six-foot leash, looked back at her and whined.

"Well, go ahead, what are you waiting for?"

He tugged on the leash. Giving him some slack, she let him wander under the trees and into the shrubbery along the chain-link fence at the back. He crept between a pair of bushes, until she could see no more than the end of his tail. "A dog with modesty. Now I've seen everything."

She found Trixie's old water bowl on a shelf in the garage and filled it. "You have to stay in here while we're unloading the car," she said before removing the leash and collar. "I wouldn't want anything to happen to you. Or to my tomato plants, for that matter." He sat in front of her, ears perked forward, and swished his tail back and forth.

"So now you're carrying on a conversation with the dog?" Nick said while lugging the first of several boxes through the front door.

"He's the smartest animal I've ever met, if you can go by the way he looks at me when I talk." Together they hauled the rest of the boxes from the SUV into the split foyer, up the left-hand stairs and into the spare bedroom.

"Now remember," Nick said on his way out, "let me know if you have any trouble with Phil. I'm a high-powered lawyer. I've got connections."

She laughed in response to his grin and shooed him out the door. In her bedroom she stripped off her shorts and T-shirt to take a shower. Only while dressing did she remember the silver necklace in her purse. She certainly didn't want to carry that around. She locked it in her jewelry box with the few valuable pieces she'd inherited from her mother and returned the key to its usual place in her top drawer under a pile of hair scrunchies.

Not wanting to leave the dog alone too long, she descended the right-hand steps to the den and walked through the laundry room to the door that connected with the garage. The dog sat where she'd left him, gazing at the door as if waiting for her to appear. "Want to go out again?" she asked. She opened the outside door and watched the animal trot around the vegetable garden in the center of the yard. Again he disappeared into the bushes, where she could only take on faith that he was performing as expected.

"Okay, I guess you can come in now. If you're smart enough not to trample the tomatoes, you can probably be trusted on the carpet." She knew he would enjoy the air-conditioning, with his alpine-evolved fur coat.

He padded after her into the dining room and lay at her feet in the computer nook while she logged on to the Internet. Accessing the website of the local paper, she placed an ad in the "Pets Found" classifieds. She didn't mention the silver necklace, which would provide a means of confirming the owner's identity. The notice would appear on the website tomorrow—Friday—and in the newspaper starting Saturday morning. "Think your master will call? He must be awfully careless, letting you run around with no tags." The dog lifted his head and emitted what sounded like a contemptuous snort.

"Hungry?" She went into the kitchen, with the dog following at her heels and poured a bowl of dry food for him.

After one sniff, he turned in a circle and lay down under the table. "Don't you dare turn up your nose at that stuff. Do you have any idea how much one bag of premium large-breed kibble costs?" The dog just lay with his head resting on his forepaws and gazed at her with his eyes rolled up—what she thought of as "whale eyes". "Okay, be that way. Starve…see if I care." Just as Vicki took a couple of boneless chicken breasts from the freezer and stuck them in the microwave to thaw, the phone rang. The second she answered it, she realized she should have waited for the machine to pick up.

Her throat tightened and her pulse accelerated at the sound of Phil's voice. She should have known getting away without confrontation would be too much to hope for. She greeted him in as casual a tone as she could manage.

"What's with this ridiculous note you left? If it's some female ploy for attention, forget it." She visualized him in his open-necked shirt and tailored slacks, with his fair-haired, square-jawed good looks that Nick always said reminded him of a cross between a golf pro and a politician.

Phil's tone grated on her nerves. Though she'd half expected to feel wistful regret for the loss of a two-year relationship, instead she felt only mild irritation, along with a desire to cut the conversation short and return to more interesting pursuits. "The last thing I want is more of your attention. Like I said in the note, we're through. I'm sorry it has to be this way but my decision is final."

He shifted from impatient to wheedling. "Come on, Vicki, whatever you're upset about, we can work it out. We both have too much invested to let it fall apart over nothing."

"Invested?" She caught herself gritting her teeth and forced her jaws to relax. "I am not a mutual fund. And I don't consider my concerns nothing. Goodbye, Phil."

Only after she hung up, with an unexpected grin on her face, did she notice the Saint Bernard growling. "It's okay, that's over." She scratched between his ears and he leaned against her, his tongue lolling out one side of his mouth. "I can't believe I was crazy about that guy once. It just dawned on me how long I've actually been tired of him. Guess I was afraid to admit to myself how much time I've wasted already." She ruffled the dog's ears. "But you wouldn't know about that, would you? With you it's love 'em and leave 'em. No complications."

The dog plopped down on the floor, his ears drooping. After taking the chicken out of the microwave, she switched on the portable radio on the counter, tuned to a country station in Washington. "I can't tell you how many times Phil ragged on me about listening to country music. He thought it was low-class or something. Well, the heck with him." Swaying to the rhythm, she chopped the meat into bite-sized pieces and heated a pan for stir-fry. "He didn't like the way I dressed, either." She wielded the knife with emphatic strokes on onions and bell peppers, the latter from her own plants. Though she didn't have a flare for gardening in general, she did enjoy growing and eating fresh vegetables. "Kept hinting I should shop at better stores and do something about my hair. Like I need to dress up for my job. I can just see myself wearing designer jeans for cats to throw up on."

The dog's eyes stayed fixed on her, his head swiveling to follow her every move. A thread of saliva drooled from his jowls. "You want my dinner, don't you? Fat chance. Maybe your owner spoiled you but don't expect me to do the same." He stared at her from those droopy brown eyes and whimpered. "Oh, all right." She tossed a chunk of chicken onto the floor and he gulped it down.

When he begged for more, though, she hardened her heart. Dr. Brodie would scold her if he knew she'd fed an animal any raw meat at all. After cooking, she did unbend enough to slip the dog a few pieces of the stir-fried chicken. He sat near her chair and watched like a vulture while she ate, with one of the cat-themed mysteries Phil dismissed as stupid propped in front of her. After supper, weakening again, she let the dog lick her plate and the frying pan before she loaded the dishwasher. After a few minutes of rummaging under the sink, she found her old grooming brush. "Come on boy, let's get that dirt out of your coat." She coaxed him into the living room, sat on the floor and patted the spot next to her. "Lie down."

He immediately stretched out on the carpet and laid his head on her knee. "You're the best-trained animal I've seen in a long time." His tail thumped when she ran the brush down his back. "What nice soft fur you've got." From the goofy doggie grin he gave her, she could almost imagine he understood the words as well as the tone. He obeyed instantly when she commanded him to roll over for brushing his other side and he even held still to have his tail and back legs groomed—a process most dogs resisted. She stroked his head, enjoying the warm weight in her lap. She'd never owned a giant breed but she found his size and solidity reassuring. She buried her fingers in his thick fur, thinking what a great hand and foot warmer he'd make on cold nights. "Except you aren't mine. You're just visiting." She rubbed his stomach, inciting one of his hind legs to twitch in the typical canine reflex.

She leaned against the front of the couch, her eyelids drooping. The dog rested his head on her lap again, looking as weary as she felt. "Can't believe I'm so tired. It's been a hectic day, I guess." Ridiculous, only old people fell asleep right after dinner. Still, she let her eyes close. *I'll rest a few minutes.*

Darkness swirled around her. A voice whispered in her ear, "Thank you for taking me in." A man's voice. Hot breath tickled her neck and raised shivers along her spine.

Chapter Two

ജ

Who are you?

"Doesn't matter. The important thing is that you saved me."

From what?

"Something I don't want to contemplate. I've found my haven with you." Lips nibbled her ear and grazed the outline of her jaw. His voice sounded familiar, though she couldn't place it.

She sighed and threw her head back to expose the hollow of her throat. A tongue flicked that sensitive spot. Her nipples puckered. *More.* Still veiled by darkness, he nuzzled the vee between her breasts. His face, lightly roughened with the beginning of a beard, rubbed the skin there and suffused it with heat.

His hands skimmed down her sides and brushed her bare legs. Her skin prickled and her nipples hardened still more. *What happened to my clothes?* Didn't matter. A disembodied lover in a black velvet cloud could touch her however he wanted.

Fingers danced up her inner thighs and, at the last second, veered away from the tender folds of her pussy, already seeping moisture and yearning for his cock. His tongue swirled around one of her nipples without quite touching it. "You smell delicious. Taste that way too."

No man had ever said that to her before. Her legs shifted in restless longing. While his fingers traced the triangle of hair on her mound, he kissed a path across her breasts, licking each nipple in turn, over the quivering flesh of her stomach, to the cleft at the apex of that triangle. "May I stay with you?" he breathed.

She arched her hips to invite a more intimate kiss. *Sure, if you keep doing that.*

"So hot—so sweet. Let me taste your cream."

Oh, yes. She opened her thighs wider. His fingers parted the folds of her pussy to make room for his tongue. It lapped up and down her slit, never quite entering and then flickered like a flame on her clit.

Her leg muscles tensed and heat engorged her pussy. A climax started building deep inside her, mounting higher every second.

The touch faded and the dark cloud melted away.

She woke up still slumped on the floor, her neck cramped from the awkward angle in which she'd fallen asleep. The pulse still throbbed between her legs. *Whoa, what brought that on? Maybe I should dig out the vibrator tonight.*

The dog lay on the carpet beside her, his ears perked forward as if curious about her odd behavior. A flush warmed her cheeks with illogical self-consciousness, as if the animal could sense the wetness in her crotch and understand what it meant. When she yawned and massaged the nape of her neck, he picked up the grooming brush in his teeth and deposited it next to her.

"No, enough of that for now. It's time for you to go in the garage. I've got work to do." He licked her hand and whined, his ears drooping. "Yeah, I like you too but I don't want you underfoot while I'm running the vacuum." She hadn't done much cleaning lately, between work and spending most of her free time at Phil's condo. It dawned on her that she'd been catering to his insecurities. How had she managed to live with his possessiveness for so long?

After escorting the dog outside and waiting for him to finish his behind-the-bushes routine, she led him into the garage and spread a threadbare quilt on the floor. She refilled the water bowl and brought out the dry food in case he got hungry enough to eat it. A fan on the workbench supplied a breeze to keep him cool. "Get some rest. You've had a rough day. I'll check on you later." He watched her with sad eyes until she went in through the laundry room and closed the door.

"Freedom," she said aloud to the empty house while vacuuming the living room. "What am I going to do with it first? Not get mixed up with another man, that's for sure. For now I'll settle for the vibrator." *And don't start talking to yourself like a dotty spinster in an old-fashioned novel, either,* she silently admonished. When she'd polished off enough housework to feel virtuous, she flopped in front of the TV with a pint of fudge ripple ice cream. What a pleasure to eat straight out of the carton without Phil casting sidelong glances at her tummy and murmuring, "Are you sure you need that?" She'd forgotten how relaxing it was not having to fight him for the remote too. He always turned on forensic detective shows when she wanted to watch the Australian guy on Animal Planet.

Oddly, she already missed the dog. It was just as well he wasn't in the room, though, because he would have begged for ice cream and chocolate was poisonous to dogs. Stowing the unfinished pint in the freezer, she went to the garage to check on him. She blinked in surprise when she switched on the overhead light.

The outside door was open. *I'm sure I locked that.* "Dog? Here, boy!" How was she supposed to call an animal whose name she didn't know? Scanning the garage, she didn't see any sign of him, not even the quilt he'd been lying on. Surely he hadn't dragged it into the yard with his teeth? It worried her that he didn't come trotting in at the sound of her voice, considering how closely he'd followed her around inside the house.

She zipped into the laundry room for a flashlight, then walked through the garage into the yard. "Here, dog! Damn it, where are you?" Growing anxiety made her voice shrill. Shining the light around, she didn't see any sign of him. The bushes by the back fence rustled, though. "Dog?" She turned the flash in that direction.

Someone called out of the dark, "Wait! Please don't look at me." A man.

Her heart raced with alarm. "Who are you? And what are you doing on my property?"

"Nobody you know. I'm sorry to bother you." He sounded vaguely familiar but the low, hoarse tone of his voice disguised most of its individuality. "Please don't look."

Ignoring his plea, she directed the beam at him. The light wavered with the trembling of her arm. She saw only a shapeless lump huddled under the quilt from her garage.

"Where's my dog? Did you let him out?" And why hadn't he barked at the intruder? Some watchdog!

"I don't know. I'm lost."

The despair in the words dispelled some of her fear. Maybe he was only a homeless man looking for refuge? If so, why didn't he hike the couple of miles downtown to the shelter? It wasn't a cold or wet night. Or was he telling the literal truth, that he was so lost he didn't know which direction downtown was? She hardened herself against the pity that might wreck her defenses. He could still be a thief or worse. "I'm calling the police."

"No, please. I won't hurt you." The pain in his voice made her nerves quiver, even as its deep pitch resonated in the pit of her stomach "This is all a mistake. I don't belong here."

"That's obvious. Why didn't you go to the homeless shelter? They might still let you in."

"I can't." The anguished whisper brought unwelcome tears to her eyes. "Don't be afraid. I'm leaving now." With surprising quickness, he scrambled over the chain-link fence, with the quilt still wrapped around him and draped over his head like a cowl.

Vicki trained the light on him but even when the cover slipped as he clambered over the fence and dropped to the other side, all she caught was a glimpse of the back of his head. In the shadows she couldn't see well enough to have any hope of identifying him if he ever came back.

And why would he? He was probably a pitiful derelict who wouldn't want to linger anywhere near a place where he might get arrested. She ignored the nagging insistence in the corner of her mind that his resonant voice, even distorted by pain, didn't sound like a street bum's. After all, educated people could wind up homeless just like dropouts.

She rushed out the front gate and around the side yard to the rear, where her lot adjoined the woods of Back Creek Nature Park. No sign of the fleeing man. Nothing but the quilt discarded on the ground.

She called the dog, panning the flashlight beam from side to side in the remote hope that if he'd wandered into the woods, he would notice her and come back. She spotted nothing except a rabbit startled by her presence and heard nothing except crickets. After zipping into the house for the leash, she wandered up and down the sidewalk, calling softly to avoid disturbing the neighbors. It was still early in the evening and a retired man who lived at the end of the block stepped outside to greet her. He hadn't seen the dog. After covering several blocks in each direction, she headed home. Rubbing at the tears that blurred her eyes, she squelched the idea of blundering through the woods in search of the dog. Amid all those acres of trees, she wouldn't have a chance. Either the dumb animal would come back on his own or he wouldn't.

The tears flowed freely by the time she got home. What would the dog's owner say about her letting him get lost? More importantly, suppose he got hit by a car or stolen for use in a dogfight? What if he did have a concussion and collapsed with nobody to tend his injuries? She crumpled onto the couch, her face buried in her arms. "No wonder I couldn't make a relationship work. I can't do anything right. I can't even keep track of a stupid dog."

* * * * *

Stefan dropped the quilt and dashed into the woods, burning with humiliation. Waking up naked on a garage floor had given him a severe shock. At first he hadn't known where he was or why. Then all the memories of the past few hours had come flooding back. His attempt to bend Diana's spell to his own purposes must have worked at least partly, since he'd become human again. But for how long? No matter how fervently he hoped for a permanent cure, he knew he couldn't count on escaping the curse that easily. The confrontation with the woman, Vicki, had jolted him with sickening disappointment. When he tried to cast a veil of invisibility over himself and she had no trouble seeing him, he felt as if he'd fallen over a cliff. Diana must have bound his powers.

He ran until his ribs ached. When he collapsed, gulping air, onto the ground, he noticed he'd scraped his feet on twigs and pebbles. His stomach roiled. The one bite of dry dog food he'd sampled when Vicki had refused to give him more chicken felt like a hard lump in his gut. He swallowed, determined not to add vomiting to the rest of his misery.

If he could retrieve his amulet, he felt confident his magic would come back with it, now that he'd had some time to recover from the onslaught of Diana's spell. But Vicki had taken off the necklace and he had no way of knowing exactly where she had stashed it. The easy solution, that she'd kept it in her purse where he could steal it back with minimal effort, seemed the least likely. She'd struck him as too conscientious for that.

Huddled under the trees with his arms wrapped around his bent legs, he mulled over every detail of the evening. His clear memories started with barreling into the side of Vicki's brother's car. Before that, all he could recall were blurred images of fleeing from Diana's basement and racing along the road, dodging cars and panting in the heat, his chest painfully heaving. From glimpses of his surroundings in the parking lot and through the car window on the way to Vicki's, he figured out he had run from Diana's house on the Annapolis Neck peninsula a couple of miles to Bay Ridge near Forest Drive. To reach his own home, a waterfront townhouse on the Eastport side of Annapolis across the creek from the historic downtown, would be an easy walk of less than an hour. Except that he couldn't go home, even if he had clothes and keys. That would be the first place Diana would search for him and until he got his powers back, he had to stay out of her clutches.

Shifting his legs to relieve the itchy sensations of pine needles and dry leaves under his buttocks, he sorted through his memories of the conditions he'd tried to attach to the spell. He'd begged to retain some humanity. He had that, for what it was worth. He'd raised a shield against hostile magic. That had apparently worked, because the bolt of energy Diana had cast at him had bounced off. He remembered asking to be sent to a place of refuge and obviously Vicki's house was it. No, not so much her home as the woman herself. His impromptu spell had created a magnetic attraction between them. Furthermore, she had been the first person to touch him after his transformation and he'd imprinted on her. He shivered at the memory of her soothing touch, her strong yet soft hands running over his canine body. And then the brief but intense dream they'd shared when he'd dozed off—only residual magic could have generated that. If he reverted to dog form, he knew he would have to return to her place for shelter but that prospect was more than a matter of necessity. He *wanted* to go back to Vicki. When he'd heard her calling in the distance a few minutes ago, he had yearned to answer, to throw himself at her feet and beg for sanctuary. That had to be a side effect of the spell. He would certainly never feel drawn to a woman that way in normal circumstances.

Heaving himself off the ground, he limped to the nearest hiking trail, where the smoother earth wouldn't hurt his feet so much. He crept to the edge of the woods and stalked parallel to the mostly fenced yards that bounded the undeveloped area. Not that he had any clear idea of where he was headed. He certainly couldn't return to the woman, not like this. She'd have him arrested. Yet his mind couldn't stop gnawing on the memory of her face and voice. Why had the magic fixated on her?

A few minutes later, the answer came to him. Now that his human brain had started functioning more or less normally, he recognized her. Vicki Lindstrom, one of the veterinary assistants at the clinic where his cat, Caesar, had been treated. They had become close, in a peculiar way, over the final year of Caesar's life. Although Stefan had never interacted with Vicki outside the medical setting until that last day, he'd come to consider her almost a friend. He'd looked forward to seeing her each time he brought the cat in for the latest round of treatments for kidney failure. And she'd offered sympathy he couldn't seek anywhere else when he'd made the decision to have the cat euthanized. He certainly wouldn't have admitted to Diana or anyone else in the coven how much that scruffy animal meant to him. He'd acquired Caesar during high school, while living with his aunt. As a cruelly misunderstood teenager, or so he'd imagined himself, he'd treated the cat as his only confidant. Just about that time, his powers had begun to surface and with no idea how to control them, he'd kept his distance from people. Only the cat seemed like a safe companion. Vicki accepted that tie to a pet as normal, where most other people would react with a tolerant smile at best. A bitter laugh escaped Stefan's lips. Of course it would take a situation like that to make him regard a woman as a friend instead of a potential bed partner. Maybe Diana had a point.

Diana. Anger flared within him. How dare she presume to punish him like a wayward adolescent, for his chosen lifestyle? His love life was none of her damn business and as soon as he regained his full powers, he would make her regret the humiliation she'd inflicted. But first he had to find that amulet.

That gave him another vital reason to hang around Vicki's place. Most likely, she had put the necklace somewhere in her bedroom. Well, getting into women's bedrooms had never posed much of a problem for him. And winning an invitation into hers would be more of a pleasure than a chore. *Hell, where did that come from?* He reminded himself that the magnetism drawing him to her sprang from the spell, not natural attraction. Although cute in a wholesome kind of way, she didn't fall into the glamorous or seductive category of his typical partners, not even magically gifted like Tanith. Again his skin twitched at the memory of Vicki's fingers scratching behind his ears and rubbing his chest. In canine form, he'd luxuriated in her attention. Now, though, having accidentally plunged into her sleeping mind for a few minutes, he could imagine how those caresses would feel on his human body. Heat flooded his loins and his face flushed. Not that he'd be likely to get the chance. She lavished affection on a lost dog but a man she hardly knew would provoke a different reaction. He wasn't used to simple affection from women. The ones he knew were divided among playmates, clients and colleagues such as other adepts. Including Diana, damn her to the Abyss!

Power such as hers and his own was rare. Most neopagans of all varieties, including their own eclectic Chaos Magic coven, had no real spell-casting ability. The minority, who regarded their rituals as more than symbolic, tended to be fooling themselves. Few of them possessed anything stronger than faint traces of clairvoyance or precognition and most of those didn't have a clue how to control their talents. Stefan had joined Diana's circle in the first place because he'd been attracted by the compatibility between their gifts. But he'd always assumed his strength surpassed hers. Discovering the extent of his self-delusion stunned him. Well, now that he knew the score, he would be prepared next time they met.

Meanwhile, he knew he couldn't waste energy brooding on his thirst for revenge. First things first. He needed clothes. Even if he wanted to take Vicki's advice and seek refuge at the homeless shelter across town on West Street—a thought that made him cringe—he couldn't go there naked. Swatting at mosquitoes, he continued along the edge of the woods, scanning each house he passed. Most had enough lights burning to give him a view, if only a dim one, of their backyards. After what seemed like an hour, he came across an unfenced lot with a deck in the rear. He noticed something draped over the stair rail. When he sneaked closer, sticking to patches of shadow under trees, he recognized the objects as a pair of swimming trunks and a T-shirt. Close to the house, he crouched down and crawled, freezing at every rustle of branches in the breeze. His face heated with shame at being stuck in this ridiculous position. Luckily, nobody heard him and came outside to challenge his intrusion. He snatched the garments from the railing, darted into the woods and tugged them on. They were damp with a clammy chill that made him shudder in contrast to the warm, humid air.

What now? He'd already decided he couldn't go home. Nor could he challenge Diana without his magic. No longer restricted to the shadows, he cut between two yards and emerged at the edge of the road. The sidewalk felt smooth under his sore feet. Without a destination in mind, he started walking toward downtown. Although he couldn't risk returning to his townhouse, heading in that direction brought irrational comfort. Maybe before he got as far as his own neighborhood, a useful idea would occur to him.

A lingering headache from the close encounter with the SUV clouded his brain and slowed his pace. He needed to rest for a few minutes. He came upon a small church set in the midst of a broad lawn with a few trees in back, off the street. Detouring toward them, he lay down in the deep shadows where nobody would notice him. The cool, moist grass lured him to relax. He lounged on his back and gazed at the moon through the branches.

First, he had to get clothes and money, a problem if he didn't want to show himself on his own street but not an insurmountable one. After that, he needed to get access to Vicki's house and search for the amulet. He remembered watching Vicki place a lost dog ad. All right, he would answer that ad in search of his wandering pet. With years of practice at charming women, he shouldn't need magic to wiggle into her good graces.

Drowsiness crept over him. It wouldn't hurt to sleep a little while, as long as he didn't get caught here in the morning. He let his eyes drift shut.

He snapped awake from a dream of Diana's power searing him like a flame. His skin prickled and a new growth sprouted from the base of his spine. His joints crackled as his bones stretched and bent into unnatural shapes.

Crawling Chaos, I'm changing back! Tears stung his eyes. Scrabbling at his clothes, he stripped them off while his fingers morphed into claws. A sob ripped from his throat. A minute later, he stood on four legs with the swimsuit and shirt in a heap underneath him.

No longer able to weep, he howled his despair. Now he had no decisions to make. Only one refuge was open to him. Picking up the clothes in his teeth, he trotted through the darkness back to Vicki's place.

Chapter Three

ꟹ

In nothing but her satin nightgown, Vicki rose from the bed and drifted downstairs without turning on any lights. When she opened the door to the garage, she caught a glimpse of movement in the shadows cast by the street lamp. A man spoke. "Please don't make me leave again. I'm lost. I have nowhere else to go."

She recognized the same voice that had caressed her ears during her brief nap earlier that evening. When his resonant bass tone sent a tingle down her spine, with no hint of fear, she realized this encounter wasn't really happening. "You aren't here. This is a dream."

"Yes," he said with a tinge of surprise. "I didn't know I could still do this, enter your dreams. Don't send me away. I need you. With you, I don't feel lost." In the darkness, his darker bulk rose to full height. He strode toward her.

Her stomach clenched but not with fear. When he reached for her hand, she let him clasp it. "May I come inside?" The words made her diaphragm vibrate like a harp string.

"Yes," she breathed. The next moment, they stood in her bedroom. Now she could make out his face, framed by black hair curling halfway down his neck. *I know him.* But she couldn't remember his name or where they'd met. *Who cares, I'm dreaming. Enjoy it while it lasts.*

He opened his arms. She stepped into their welcoming circle, which closed around her. With a shock, she realized he was naked. His half-erect cock nudged her stomach and incited a trickle of warmth between her legs. His hands roamed up and down her back, molding her body to his. Nestling into the hollow of his shoulder, she found that his chin rested comfortably on the top of her head. "I thought I'd have to wander in the dark forever," he said, his chest rumbling under her ear. The drumbeat of his heart echoed in her head.

"You're safe here," she whispered. Why did she feel impelled to comfort this stranger?

"I know." He stroked her hair. "I knew the moment I saw you. You're too kind to cast me out." His fingers crept under her hair to massage the nape of her neck. "I needed shelter and you offered it."

"Glad to help." Although she didn't know what he was talking about, the words made her melt inside anyway. She skimmed her hands over his back and traced the firm contours of his butt.

He retaliated by kneading her derriere. "Soft," he murmured. The guttural tone of suppressed need, combined with the pressure of his fingers, sent tingles through her most sensitive places.

Her nipples stiffened at the friction of his skin through her satin gown, the material so thin that the crisp hairs on his chest tickled her. The hard ridge of his shaft pressed more urgently against the pit of her stomach. The heat radiating from that spot made liquid well up between her thighs. Without conscious thought, she stood on tiptoe, trying to rub her pussy against his cock. Her clit was already thickening, eager for contact.

With a deep-pitched chuckle, he clutched her hips more tightly and rocked forward to achieve that contact. "Is this what you want?"

She hid her face on his shoulder, her cheeks scorching. "You know it."

"How about this?" He reached under her nightgown and rolled it up inch by inch, his hands sliding up the backs of her thighs to her bare bottom. Involuntarily her nails dug into his flesh. A groan escaped from him. "You've got claws like a kitten. If I pet your pussy, will you purr?"

A flood of heat washed over her. "Try me."

One hand roamed around her hip to the front and slipped between their bodies to cup the triangle above her slit. He stroked the hair without quite touching the cleft that begged for attention. She moaned.

"That's it," he said with that same hint of laughter. "Purr for me."

"More," she gasped. "My clit needs rubbing." In real life she could never imagine saying such a thing out loud.

"What about my need?" His cock jutted against her.

She gripped it and rubbed up and down. Glancing down, she watched the head swell and darken, engorged with blood. He parted the folds of her pussy and caressed the swollen bud.

"You welcomed me into your sanctuary," he said. "Will you invite me into this haven too?" His other hand reached between her thighs from behind and skimmed over her wet slit.

"Oh, yes. Anytime." Her clit was already starting to pulse. She spread her legs and braced them to allow him deeper access. Automatically her hand continued pumping his shaft. She circled the tip with her thumb and felt a drop of moisture ooze out.

He groaned and thrust into her hand. "Look at me," he said. "I want to watch your face while I make you come."

She threw her head back to gaze at him. Shadows veiled his face, yet his eyes gleamed like a wild animal's.

One finger insinuated itself into her pussy. Another strummed her clit until the vibrations resonated through her whole body. She clung to him, shuddering, while his lips grazed her nipples. Again he lifted his head to stare into her eyes. "Come for me." He found the burning spot at the tip of her clit that begged for attention and rubbed faster and faster while she rocked in time with his strokes. The glow in his eyes flared hotter when her climax crashed over her. He smiled in satisfaction before bending to run his tongue in slow spirals around her breasts once more.

How can he be that flexible? Silly question, she decided. In a fantasy, anything could happen.

"Now, let me in," he demanded.

She opened her legs still wider. He slipped his arms under her thighs and lifted her to impale her on his cock. Now she was the one performing improbable feats. Never especially limber, she wrapped her legs around his waist and locked herself in position with no effort. Her arms twined around his neck. His mouth captured hers, their tongues darting together while he surged to the hilt within her.

Long after she should have run out of breath, she broke off the kiss and murmured into his neck, "No protection?"

"This is a dream, remember? No condoms needed."

"Oh, yeah," she said muzzily. "I'm on the Pill anyway." Of course, if she was awake, she would've had to worry about disease, but nothing like that could happen in a dream.

With a growl, he rocked his hips, urging her to move with him. She gazed into his eyes while he slid in and out, slowly at first, each stroke long and deliberate. She whimpered at the torment of the friction deep inside on her G-spot. Her inner muscles began to contract around his cock. His eyes smoldered like live coals. His thrusts goaded her to a second peak, then to a third while her sheath still rippled from the aftershocks.

"Come with me!" she cried.

His strokes grew harder and faster. Clinging with both arms and legs tightly wrapped around his body, she rocked in perfect harmony with him. The motion felt like flying, yet with no danger of a fall. He closed his eyes as he drove toward his climax. His breath rasped through parted lips. At last, roaring aloud, he clasped her to him and shuddered through his release. To her amazement, she soared to one last peak with him.

Somehow she found herself lying on the bed, his body covering hers. "Thank you," he murmured, his hot breath on the pulse point in her throat. He lifted his head to gaze at her. "I don't feel lost now." Then the warmth of his embrace faded and the vision of his eyes gazing raptly at her splintered into an iridescent mist.

* * * * *

Vicki woke to the sound of barking. For a second she mistook it for part of the dream. No, it definitely came through the window she'd opened when she'd turned off the air conditioner before falling asleep. After she dragged herself out of bed and to the bathroom, the noise was still going on. Dressed only in a nightgown, she slid her feet into flip-flops and hurried downstairs to the garage. When she opened the outside door leading to the backyard, she found the dog sitting there.

At the sight of her, he leaped up, tail wagging frantically. "Oh, God, where on earth have you been?" She knelt and flung her arms around his neck, tears streaming down her cheeks. His tongue lapped her face. She giggled through her tears. "Yuck, dog breath! Bad boy, don't even think about running away again. Get in the house right this minute." With a quick glance at the front gate, she noticed it stood ajar. That strange man must have left it open, a fact that explained the dog's escape and return. Still lashing the white plume of his tail from side to side, he followed her into the garage, where he emptied the water bowl in a few gulps. After tossing out the leftover kibble, she refilled the dish. The dog turned around and sat facing away from the food.

"Again? I've never seen an animal with such picky tastes. What does your master feed you, steak? Oh, all right, come in the house." He paced at her side and lay on her bedroom floor while she dressed. He watched her so intently that she blushed. "What are you staring at? Come on, time for breakfast."

In the kitchen, when she poured herself a bowl of granola, the dog whined and pawed at her with a heavy forefoot. "Let me guess, you want cereal too." Although she knew better than to reinforce begging behavior, she was so relieved to have him back that she couldn't resist his pleas. She fixed him a bowl of granola with milk too, followed by a piece of toast. He sat at her feet to keep her company while she ate an English muffin. "I draw the line at giving you orange juice. You wouldn't like it anyway." He plopped his head onto her lap. She stroked him while glancing through the morning paper.

"I have to get to work and you have to go in the garage." His brown eyes gazed into hers and he emitted a squeaky whine that sounded odd coming from that huge chest. "Sorry, you can't stay loose in the house by yourself and after what happened last night, I'm not about to let you wander around the yard." Even though she felt certain he must have escaped through the open gate, now carefully latched, she didn't want to take the risk of leaving him out all day. After locking him in with food, water, the fan and the quilt, she headed for the clinic.

Shelly, a dark-haired, blue-eyed college student who worked in the office part-time, was staffing the front desk when Vicki went in. "I heard about the dog that followed you home," she said with a grin. "How is he?"

"Seems fine now." When Dr. Brodie asked her the same question a minute later, she gave the same answer, without mentioning the incident of the night before. She didn't want to sound careless. The dog had come back, so no permanent harm was done. She told both of the vets on duty about the ad she'd placed. At their suggestion, she printed up a notice for the bulletin board in the waiting room.

In the middle of the morning, Shelly called her to the desk to answer the phone. Vicki's shoulders sagged when she heard Phil's voice. "What are you doing calling me here?"

"I figured you wouldn't pick up if I phoned you at home."

"Well, you got that right. Listen, I'm busy and we have nothing to discuss."

His tone hardened. "Don't you blow me off. We have plenty to discuss and we can do it at dinner tonight. If you're trying to teach me a lesson or some crap like that, okay, you've had enough time."

She sighed. "I'm not going with you to dinner or anywhere else." To think she'd been excited by his take-charge manner when they'd started dating. When he'd sprung plans on her without checking first, she'd enjoyed the swept-off-her-feet exhilaration. Now, like most of his other traits, she found it infuriating. "And don't call me at work again." She hung up in the middle of his spluttered retort.

Shelly gave her a smile and a thumbs-up. "You go, girl."

"Sorry about the interruption. Don't accept any more calls from him."

On her lunch hour she drove home, a trip of less than five minutes, to let out the dog. She was relieved to find him right where she'd left him. *Where else would he be, for heaven's sake? He can't open the door by himself.* He greeted her with ecstatic wiggling and tail-wagging. She ruffled his fur, reveling in the solid muscle rippling under his coat. After he visited the bushes, she let him trot around the yard for a few minutes while she gathered ripe tomatoes and cucumbers. He emitted a sharp yelp when a squirrel darted past him and up a tree. He stopped short and glanced back at Vicki, almost as if apologizing for the squirrel-chasing impulse.

At one point she noticed him settle on his haunches and scratch behind an ear. "Good grief, I hope you aren't getting fleas. I don't have any way of knowing whether you've had the treatment." He crowded through the door alongside her when she went into the kitchen to put the vegetables away. "If you think you're staying in here, you have another think coming. I have to go back to the office."

He sat next to her and leaned his weight against her leg. "Stop trying to look pitiful." When she rubbed behind his ears, his eyelids drooped in a sensual daze. "Playtime's over. Back in the garage." She had to give him a shove to get him moving in the right direction.

At the clinic she bought a package of flea-repellent medication. The vet assured her that even if the dog had already been treated that month, one extra dose wouldn't hurt him. Shelly mentioned that Vicki's "significant other" had phoned again while she was gone.

"He isn't that anymore, thank goodness."

"Well, I told him to quit calling."

When she got home in the late afternoon, she found the dog waiting to greet her with the same enthusiasm as before. "Wow, nobody else is ever that glad to see me," she said as she let him into the yard. Less pleasantly, she found a message from Phil on the answering machine. After the first five words of his rant, she deleted the recording. At her side, the dog growled deep in his chest. "I can see you're an excellent judge of character. Don't worry, he won't bother us anymore."

Her temporary pet squirmed when she snipped the end off the tube of flea repellent oil. She'd noticed before that animals didn't like the drops. The medication must have an odor human noses couldn't perceive. She had to lie practically on top of him, sprawled on the kitchen floor, to massage the oil into the top of his head. "See, that wasn't so bad." While she brushed dog hair off her shirt, he shook himself and cast a reproachful look at her. Having decided feeding him kibble was a waste of time, she thawed two packages of hamburger in the microwave.

"Yep, I don't know why it took me so long to notice what a jerk Phil was," she said as she browned the first batch of meat. "We met at some political thing Nick took me along to. A Christmas party, that's what it was. I guess Phil got the wrong impression, seeing me in makeup and a cocktail dress with my hair styled." She gave her shoulder-length ponytail a flip. The dog stared at her as if absorbing every word, though more likely he was concentrating on the aroma of the ground beef. "If that's what he thought he was getting, no wonder he acted like he'd been cheated when he got to know the real me." She gestured at the jeans and casual blouse she wore. "What you see is what you get. I was never much for dating in high school or even after that. I spent more time collecting bugs and dragging home stray cats than trying to impress guys."

She drained the grease from the pan and scooped the meat onto a plate. Saliva drooled from the dog's open mouth. "Calm down, you have to wait for it to cool." With the country music station playing in the background, she molded the second batch of hamburger into patties seasoned with chopped onion. "He seemed totally nice at first. Maybe I wasn't paying attention to his real personality because I wasn't used to having that kind of money spent on me. I got a kick out of the fancy restaurants, not to mention all those concerts and plays in Washington. When the sarcastic zingers started, I thought they were funny at first. But pretty soon they got old." She set the plate of ground beef on the floor and the dog attacked it like a starving bear after a winter of hibernation. "He sniped at my clothes, my hair, my waistline, my taste in books and music, you name it. And when I asked him why the heck he was going out with me if that was how he felt, he claimed he was joking and ragged on me for being too sensitive."

The dog licked the last crumbs from the plate and flicked his tail as if answering her comments. He lay under the table while she fixed her burgers, garnished with sliced tomatoes from the garden and sat down to eat with the newspaper open on the table. "When he started thinking he could run my life, I decided I was fed up with him. Trying to make me sell my house! Not just suggesting, practically ordering." The dog listened with his head cocked and ears perked. She resisted the impulse to toss a bite of her burger to him. Feeding pets at the table had never been allowed in her family. When she served herself a bowl of vanilla ice cream, though, she did allot a scoop to her canine guest. He made it vanish in two slurps.

She opened a bottle of white zinfandel, poured a glass and carried it into the living room to watch a nature program about wolf packs. "Look what wonderful parents your cousins are. And how loyal they are to their mates." The dog thumped his tail on the rug in agreement. She swallowed a hearty gulp of the wine. "Too bad most human males aren't like that. I almost wish I could keep you. You'd probably make a better companion than the average guy."

The dog laid his head on her knees and licked the hand that rested in her lap. She stroked the velvety fur of his ears and muzzle. With a sigh, he rolled his eyes to gaze up at her. To her dismay, tears started trickling down her cheeks. The dog whimpered as if in sympathy.

She swiped her hand across her eyes. "Don't worry, I'm okay. I'm not crying over dumb old Phil. Just disappointed that the prince turned into a frog, I guess." She emptied her wineglass in one long swig. "All girls want to believe in the fairytale, right? But I should've been old enough to know better." She rubbed the soft fur of the dog's chest. "Who would've guessed I had such lousy judgment? Too bad men aren't as easy to figure out as animals. How am I supposed to know if the next one is a keeper or another toad wearing a prince costume?"

The dog gave her hand another lick, then stood up and paced toward the stairs leading down to the foyer. "What's up, boy?" He looked back at her and whined. "Want to go out?" She let him lead her downstairs and through the den to the laundry room. "Okay, outside." When she took him through the garage into the yard, he immediately dashed behind the bushes next to the fence. With twilight closing in, the shadows hid him from sight.

She laughed. "All right, I get it, you're shy. You know, you're the strangest dog I've ever met." When he didn't reappear after a minute or two, she whistled. No response. She knew she would have noticed if he'd jumped the fence, so she wasn't worried. "Hide all you want. See if I care. I'll bring you inside in a few minutes." She went back to the living room, poured another glass of wine and curled up in front of the TV.

At the next commercial, she realized she hadn't heard a sound from the dog since putting him out. She ran out the front door and checked the gate first. Definitely shut. A whistle brought no reaction from the dark corners of the yard. "Where are you, boy? I know you've got to be here someplace, right?" No rustle in the shrubbery, no galumphing, tail-waving beast. "Not again! Don't do this to me, dog."

She worked her way along the fence, shoving branches out of the way and calling in a low voice. When she'd traced the entire perimeter of the yard, she had to admit that the animal wasn't going to pop up from under a bush. *So I was wrong. He did jump the fence, after all, maybe both times.* With the flashlight, she roamed up and down the block for twenty minutes but with little hope. He had obviously dashed off to wherever he'd gone the night before. She could only wait and see whether he'd return on his own the same way.

Or maybe I should hope he doesn't. He's getting to be more trouble than he's worth. Let his owner worry about him. But the cold lump in her chest contradicted that thought.

* * * * *

In canine form, Stefan trotted into the woods to the fallen log under which he'd stashed his stolen clothes. At the instant of nightfall, he felt the energy of transformation tingling along his nerves. So the restlessness that had seized him at twilight meant what he'd hoped. He could expect to turn human every night as darkness fell and transform back into a dog somewhere around midnight. Standing upright, he stretched his arms and absently scratched the mosquito bite on his neck. One good thing among many about losing the dog shape, he couldn't smell the astringent odor of the medicinal drops anymore. As an animal, of course he couldn't explain to Vicki that he wasn't scratching at a flea.

Vicki. His cock stirred at the memory of the dream they'd shared. He hadn't completely gotten over the shock of discovering his lucid dreaming ability remained intact. Probably because it fell into a different category of gifts—many people without a trace of any other type of magic or psychic power could master that skill. More surprising, though, was that he'd been able to project himself into Vicki's dreaming mind. On top of that, it had happened spontaneously, without any conscious intention, a detail that scared him a little. It must have something to do with the magnetism his hastily cast counter spell had forged between them. Could he repeat the act on purpose and use it to retrieve the amulet? If he couldn't find out where she'd hidden the necklace any other way, he might try interrogating her in a dream. *Diana punished me for being a callous seducer. Fine, I'll seduce my way out of this mess.*

What he really wanted, though, was to see Vicki's lush body in his waking hours, as a man rather than a dog. In animal form, he'd found the aroma of her cunt merely interesting. Remembering it now, as a man, he couldn't help craving the scent and flavor of it. He wanted that taste in real life, not only in dreams. A distracting tingle zapped through his loins as he remembered scanning her naked curves while she'd dressed that morning. She had perky tits that would fit his hands perfectly, not to mention a great ass.

Considering he had only a few hours each night to work on her, he might have to resort to a dream conversation. Bitterness at his predicament welled up in his throat like acid. Tugging on the grubby T-shirt and swimming trunks, he reminded himself that he was lucky he'd been able to subvert the spell as much as he had. Better to revert to humanity for a four-hour respite in twenty-four than to be furry full-time.

He flushed with embarrassment at the memory of barking at that squirrel in Vicki's yard. Lucky he did have these hours as a man to hang onto, because otherwise he might lapse into instinctive canine reactions more often. Eventually they might obliterate his rational self altogether.

He jogged up the road to the church where he'd rested the night before and sat on the lawn rehashing his options. He couldn't introduce himself to Vicki looking like this. First, he had to get at his assets somehow without attracting Diana's attention. He mentally tallied the friends he could rely on and came up with zero. If asked forty-eight hours earlier, he might have identified the other coven members as friends. More honestly, though, they counted as no more than colleagues. The men were, at best, friendly rivals and most of the women were ex-lovers. He couldn't think of one he could be sure of trusting not to betray him to Diana. He didn't know any of his clients well enough to appeal to them in a crisis. Those categories exhausted his list of social contacts.

What about neighbors? Faces he greeted with vague smiles at the condo association meetings. Lying back on the cool grass, he thought of one possible exception. Cliff, the owner of the townhouse next to Stefan's, had a spare key because he'd fed and medicated Caesar on the rare occasions Stefan had traveled on business. Stefan had asked him to keep the key after the cat's death in case the burglar alarm went off or some other crisis occurred while Stefan was away and he held Cliff's extra key to return the favor. Not exactly a close buddy but a potential source of help anyway.

He strolled to a shopping strip in the next block over from the church, gritting his teeth and ignoring the glances of people who noticed his smudged shirt and bare feet. Fortunately, a phone booth stood outside the barber shop and he had his calling card code memorized. In another welcome stroke of luck, Cliff was home and answered on the third ring.

"Hey, man, I'm in a little trouble. Could you do me a favor?" Magic would come in handy at this moment, to give his neighbor a small nudge toward helping him with no questions asked. On the other hand, if his power were functioning, he wouldn't be in this jam in the first place.

"Sure, what's up?"

"Woman trouble. It's too embarrassing to explain." That claim was true enough, as far as it went. Stefan had no trouble injecting a note of self-conscious hesitation into his voice. It echoed his actual feelings closely enough. "I can't go home right now. Long story. Do you have time to meet me and bring some stuff from my place?"

A chuckle, quickly suppressed. "Where?"

Stefan identified the shopping center he was calling from. "I'll meet you in front of the bank."

"No problem. What do you need?"

"Shirt, pants, shoes, a couple of sets of underwear and socks and a credit card." He described where he kept his spare cards, adding a mental expression of thanks that he didn't make a habit of carrying all the plastic he owned in his wallet.

"Clothes, huh? Man, that story you don't want to tell must be really something."

"Laugh it up, I deserve it." And he did. How could he have been so stupid as to let his guard down on Diana's home turf? He thought of asking for his extra set of car keys, in order to retrieve the car he'd left in front of her house, but reluctantly decided not to take that risk. Surely she would be watching for him to try that. He also considered asking Cliff to bring another magical focus object but two objections squelched that idea. Stefan's skin crawled at the idea of having anyone else, even someone oblivious to their power, touching those possessions most intimately tied to him. Also, explaining why he urgently needed a polished stone or an item of jewelry would raise even more awkward questions.

"I'll be there in fifteen minutes, okay?" Cliff said.

"Great. I owe you big."

For the next few minutes he rested on a bench outside the closed barber shop. When a police car patrolling the lot slowed down and the officer stared at him through the window, he got up and walked briskly along the row of stores as if he had a destination. Just before reaching a barbecued rib place near the end of the strip, he turned around and paced in the other direction to avoid the arriving and departing customers. Every casual glance thrown at him felt like ants crawling up his arms. Having people mistake him for a vagrant clashed painfully with the treatment his designer clothes and platinum cards usually earned.

Since he didn't have a watch, he couldn't confirm the impression that it took more like thirty minutes than fifteen before the car he'd been watching for pulled into a space outside the bank. The knot in his chest slackened. Cliff, a tall man with mahogany skin and graying dreadlocks, got out and strode toward him carrying a gym bag.

"Thanks, you've saved my life." Stefan took the bag and unzipped it to glance inside. "Great. Can I ask one more favor? Could you give me a lift downtown?"

Cliff pointedly surveyed his scanty outfit. "Sure. But I'd love to hear this story you don't want to tell."

As they got into the car, Stefan said, "Maybe sometime," and attempted a rakish smile that hinted at amorous adventures. If he ever got cornered into recapping this night over a couple of beers, he could have a plausible tale concocted by then.

Five minutes later, they crossed the small drawbridge over Spa Creek into downtown Annapolis. Stefan had already put on his shoes, grateful for that vital emblem of respectability. Asking Cliff to wait in front of a hotel near City Dock, he hurried into the lobby to check on vacancies. Finding that a room was available, he repeated his thanks to Cliff and returned inside to register.

Once Stefan got settled in and took a shower, the past forty-eight hours seemed like a nightmare. Lying on a king-size bed in a luxurious suite, secure in the possession of a pocketful of twenty-dollar bills from the ATM in the lobby, not to mention his credit card and clean clothes, he could hardly believe he would change into an animal within three hours. He couldn't fool himself that this reprieve was more than temporary, though. He would have the refuge of this room during his brief human hours each night but he still had to solve the problem of breaking the curse.

To accomplish that goal, he needed to get into Vicki's good graces as a man, not just a dog. That amulet had to be somewhere in her bedroom. Tonight he would call in answer to the ad. Tomorrow evening, as soon as he changed back, he would visit her in search of his lost pet. He felt a warm glow in the pit of his stomach at the thought of seeing her again. What an idiot that ex-boyfriend of hers must be. Stefan wouldn't want to change a thing about her luscious curves and auburn-streaked chestnut ponytail. His brain conjured up a ghost memory of the honeysuckle fragrance of her perfume and the sun-warmed scent of her skin, which had ravished his canine senses like flashes of color and bursts of music.

Although he felt sick at the thought of reverting to dog form, he discovered he looked forward to Vicki's voice and touch. In canine form, with an acceptable excuse to lick her hands, he'd also enjoyed her taste, a blend of salt, soap, rosewater lotion and traces of the hamburger she'd cooked. He could rationalize that as a stray dog he had no other safe place to go or that he could use the hours in her house to search for the necklace. But he had to admit to himself that his longing for contact with her gave him an even stronger motivation to return.

He flipped through the room service menu, scanning the dinner entrees while considering his strategy. Spending the days with her in canine shape did pose another problem. He would have to sneak out every night before dark before the transformation back to human form overtook him. Now that he'd vanished twice, she would exercise special care to keep him from escaping again. The sooner he found that necklace, the fewer times he would have to give her the slip.

He picked up the phone and ordered dinner. Real food, served on a plate with silverware and a napkin. He hadn't appreciated that pleasure enough when he'd had it routinely three times a day. After he ate, he would stroll up the half-mile, brick-paved stretch of Main Street to buy extra clothes before the shops closed for the night. He hadn't wanted to ask Cliff to bring more than one outfit, for fear of provoking unanswerable questions. Next, maybe he'd have a few drinks in a bar. By then the Friday night downtown crowds of tourists and midshipmen should have thinned. Or he might watch a movie in the hotel room. Anything to distract himself from brooding on what would happen at midnight. Before then, he would have to stash a set of clothes in the waterproof gym tote under a bush in the woods and sneak into Vicki's yard. He would have to brace himself for spending another twenty hours as a homeless dog.

If he were a real dog, she would gladly adopt him. He gave a dry laugh at the idea of leading the rest of his life as her pet. Feeling her rub his stomach and scratch behind his ears would offer some compensation for dull food and humiliating bathroom arrangements. But it would be more fun to savor those caresses in human form. He could think of several other places he'd like her to rub. His cock tightened at the memory of that dream. *Down, boy. Not a chance.* Not in his waking hours, anyway. Once he recovered the amulet, her temporary pet would vanish from her life and Stefan would have to do the same. Explaining why he no longer had the dog, after claiming ownership of the animal she'd rescued, would pose awkward complications. Too bad he hadn't snatched at the chance to date her after his cat's death. He'd asked but she had turned him down because of that guy she'd been involved with. Come to think of it, Stefan wondered why he hadn't used magic to undermine her reluctance. Because he didn't want to take unfair advantage of a woman who'd shown him kindness? He snorted to himself. That didn't sound like him at all.

Shaking his head to dislodge the invading swarm of strange thoughts, he got dressed. As soon as his dinner came, he would eat quickly and go out to enjoy being human while he could. Tomorrow evening would be soon enough to rent a car. At least, he reassured himself, this whole nightmare would end in a day or two. He looked forward to forgetting every detail of it, even if that had to include Vicki Lindstrom.

He sternly reminded himself of that inevitable necessity as he opened the phone book in search of her number.

* * * * *

The phone rang just as Vicki stepped out of the shower. Wrapped in a towel, she answered the call in the bedroom.

"Hello? You placed an ad about a lost dog?"

His voice, as smooth and rich as the topping on a hot fudge sundae, sounded familiar. It also gave her a ridiculous urge to pull the towel higher and tighter, as if he could see her over the phone. She felt a blush warm her face. "Yes, that was me.

"I think you might have found my Saint Bernard. My name is Stefan Rigatos."

Heat flooded her whole body. Now she realized who had invaded her dreams. This man.

Chapter Four

"Hey, I know you!" She blushed again upon hearing herself blurt out that remark. "I mean, we've met a few times. You used to bring your cat to the vet's office where I work. I'm Vicki Lindstrom." His image filled her mind's eye in three-dimensional living color—a tall man with curly black hair and olive skin. More importantly, she recalled the surprisingly gentle way he'd held his elderly tomcat still for shots and blood tests.

"Of course I remember you. What a neat coincidence. Now I know my dog's in good hands. May I come over and take a look tomorrow evening?"

"Sure, that would be fine." She wondered why he didn't make the appointment earlier. If she owned that magnificent animal, she would be in a hurry to get him back. Well, maybe the man had a full schedule on Saturday. None of her business. She gave him directions to her house.

"Excellent, I'll be there a little after eight, if that's okay."

She murmured an incoherent farewell and hung up. The last time they'd met, his cat had just been put to sleep after a long struggle with kidney failure. She'd taken a break from the office to share coffee with Stefan and he'd asked her to dinner. Even then, determined to keep her commitment to Phil, she'd been tempted by the offer. If Stefan invited her out now, she would probably accept.

No, I wouldn't, because I'm swearing off men until I get my head together. She turned back to the bathroom, vigorously rubbing her face with the towel as if that act could erase temptation from her brain. *It's not going to happen. He'll take his dog home and that'll be the end of it.* Sighing, she ran her fingers through her hair. *If I can find the dumb animal, that is.*

* * * * *

When she stumbled, half awake, into the backyard on Saturday morning, Vicki didn't know whether to laugh or scream upon finding the dog outside the garage door. The food and water bowls she'd left out "just in case" looked untouched.

"Where have you been? You're trying to drive me crazy, aren't you? It's a plot." She wondered whether he'd disappeared at the same time both nights because he had another benefactor who fed him at that hour. That pattern wasn't unusual for roaming animals. Could he even be returning to his original home? She decided the second theory didn't make sense, for in that case his owner would make sure he didn't leave again. Not only that—if the dog actually belonged to Stefan Rigatos, he wouldn't have phoned in answer to the ad when his pet had already come home once.

She continued scolding the dog while she replaced the kibble with a fresh batch and poured milk over it. With that flavoring, he ate most of the bowl, though he didn't look enthusiastic about it. "You're going to turn me into a babbling nervous wreck. I am not going to take the chance of you being gone when your master shows up." Before leaving for her half-day of Saturday work, she locked the dog in the garage again.

When she came home at one in the afternoon, he greeted her with a reproachful sigh. Ruffling his fur, she laughed at her own relief over finding him right where she'd left him. "I'm being silly, right? There's no way you could open a locked door."

A message waited on the phone. When Vicki punched the button, a woman's voice said, "I think you must have found my lost dog. Please call me as soon as possible."

Strange. How many stray Saint Bernards could be wandering around this area? She knew they weren't common locally. Her bosses' practice had only two patients of that breed. Still, two different people could conceivably have lost dogs of that description. Her canine guest might not be Stefan Rigatos' pet after all. While staring at the phone in puzzled contemplation, she became aware of a low rumble in the background. She glanced down to find the dog at her side, growling, with the fur bristling on his back. "Take it easy, boy. Nobody's here. It was just the voice mail."

She phoned the number on the recording and the woman asked to come over right away. "I've had one call about the Saint Bernard already," Vicki said, "but you're welcome to drop by and check him out."

During the conversation, the dog started growling again. Vicki smoothed his spiked hair until it lay flat. "What's wrong with you? You've acted totally friendly so far, so what's with this reaction to a phone call?" Worried about his mood, she shut him in the garage while she waited.

The doorbell rang no more than fifteen minutes later. A blonde with the height and slenderness of a fashion magazine model stood on the porch. Her face looked as if it had never wrinkled with either a frown or a laugh and her sleek cap of hair was clearly styled, not just cut. She threw a dubious glance at the giant crab before introducing herself. "Hello, I'm Diana Morrigan." She offered a hand. Her manicured fingernails matched the burgundy of her lipstick.

"Hi, I'm Vicki Lindstrom. Come on in." Conscious of her own hastily combed hair and color-free lips and nails, she stepped aside and waved the visitor into the living room. As Ms. Morrigan took a seat on the couch, Vicki reminded herself that the woman's flawlessly sculpted hairstyle, crisply tailored slacks and silk blouse didn't justify disliking her on sight. Not even if the dog had freaked at the sound of her voice.

"When did your dog go missing?"

"Thursday afternoon. I live not far from here, on the Annapolis Neck peninsula, so it seems likely he's the dog you found."

"That makes sense." She couldn't help wishing it didn't. She didn't want this woman to take her dog away. *Not my dog. Focus!* "I noticed he didn't have a tag. What's his name?"

"Rover," she said, "because he wanders off so much. He doesn't like to be tied down." Her voice held a hint of sarcasm, though her face showed no expression.

"Then I'm really surprised he wasn't wearing any ID, if he makes a habit of doing this."

"I'd taken off his collar because I was getting ready to bathe him. He escaped. You know how animals often resist what's good for them." Her lips curled in a tight smile as if some private joke amused her.

"Yeah, I hear you. I work in a vet's office." The explanation sounded flimsy. A pet owner who could afford that outfit could also afford to have a microchip implanted for her animal's safety. Furthermore, why would she take off the collar and leave on a piece of jewelry bizarrely unsuitable for canine wear? Ms. Morrigan's failure to mention the necklace gave Vicki second thoughts. She was starting to doubt the dog she'd found belonged to this woman after all.

"Then you can understand how concerned I've been. I can't wait to take him home. Where is he?" Her cool tone, tinged with what sounded like sly amusement, didn't fit the words.

"He's in the garage. Wait here and I'll bring him up." Leading the dog into the visitor's presence would quickly settle the question of whether he belonged to her.

Vicki went downstairs and let the dog in through the laundry room. "Well, your mistress is here. Or so she claims. Looks like this might be goodbye."

He halted in his tracks and tilted his head to look up at her. When she twined her fingers in the ruff at the back of his neck to urge him to move on, he resisted, a faint rumble in his throat.

"Don't be like that. I'll bet she's been worried sick about you." *Not that she sounded very upset.* Vicki gave the dog's fur another tug and started walking. He trotted along with her.

As soon as they reached the top of the steps leading into the living room, he stopped short again. Ms. Morrigan stood up. "Oh, yes, that's Rover. I can't thank you enough for taking care of him." She took a leash out of her purse.

The dog froze with his eyes riveted on her. His lips curled back from his fangs. A snarl vibrated in his chest and slowly rose in volume.

With a tight smile, the woman said, "Now, Rover, what's gotten into you? It's time to go home."

Her saccharine tone did nothing to soothe him. When she took a step closer, his growl built to a crescendo. The fur on his neck and all the way down his back bristled. Vicki's pulse raced. She edged away from the animal, afraid of him for the first time. "I haven't seen him act like this before."

Ms. Morrigan reached toward him, the leash dangling from her hand. "He's just confused, poor thing." His ears flattened against his skull.

"Maybe you should leave for now." Vicki swallowed to ease the dryness in her throat.

The woman frowned for a second before her face smoothed to cool detachment again. "You don't believe this is my dog?"

"I'm not doubting you," she said insincerely, "but you can see how upset he is. Forcing him to go with you in this mood doesn't seem like a good idea." The dog's body quivered as if fighting the urge to lunge at the intruder. "I'd feel awful if he bit you."

"Maybe you're right." Ms. Morrigan made a loop of the leash and began braiding the two halves of its length together. The weaving motion drew Vicki's eyes. She gazed at the pattern with a fascination that puzzled her. The strap seemed to glitter, surely an illusion, because it was made of leather, with no metal other than the latch at the end. On the threshold of audibility, she heard the woman humming. Or crooning a song with no recognizable words.

Vicki's eyelids drooped. Her head seemed to float a foot above her body. A voice whispered, "You want to be rid of this animal. Put on the leash and let me take him."

"Mm-hmm." She held out her hand. Something nudged her leg. Jarred, she shook her head. "No, can't do that."

The song in the background grew louder. Its music swirled around her like a perfumed whirlpool bath. She wanted to sink into its foaming heat.

Something butted into her, harder this time. The shock snapped her out of the daze. Her head jerked up to confront the woman's icy gray eyes.

"The dog. Give him to me."

The pulse pounded in Vicki's temples. Her windpipe tightened as if fingers of iron squeezed her throat. She had to make it stop, had to do what the voice ordered. Again she reached for the leash.

A third time, a solid body rammed into her. The pressure that compressed the air around her released like a bursting balloon. She stumbled over the dog and landed on the rug in an awkward heap, leaning on one elbow. He loomed over her with his teeth bared at the woman.

Ms. Morrigan hissed like an angry cat and retreated a step. Draping an arm over the dog's back for support, Vicki pulled herself to her feet. When she stood upright and looked straight at the woman, the previous cool smile had replaced the glare.

"Yes, I do believe you're right, after all. It wouldn't be wise to try to force him to go with me now." The leash vanished into her purse and she took out a business card. "Take your time and think about it. Here's my number. Call me as soon as you decide." She handed over the card and marched down the steps to the foyer and out the door.

Stunned, Vicki clutched the banister at the top of the half-staircase. Her knees wobbled. The remnants of a headache lurked behind her eyes. *What just happened? Am I coming down with the flu or something? Or did that weird woman try to hypnotize me?* A warm, wet tongue lapped her wrist. Glancing down, she saw the dog sitting calmly, his ears perked and his fur smooth. She eyed him dubiously. "What was all that about? Now you've got me wondering if you're dangerous."

Tongue lolling from one side of his mouth, he rubbed his head against her thigh. "Yeah, I have to admit you don't look it now." From all she'd learned in her job, she knew she ought to turn him over to animal control immediately. Trusting a potentially ferocious dog was the height of foolishness. Yet her instincts insisted that he wasn't dangerous to her. She couldn't stand the thought of having him locked up, maybe destroyed. He'd behaved tamely enough with everyone else. "You just don't like her, do you?" She ruffled his head. "Is your name Rover?"

The dog turned his back on her and lay down.

"Nope, I didn't think so. But you do know that woman, I bet. Why would you hate her so much if you didn't? Did she hurt you?" Vicki's first thought had been that her visitor was simply mistaken, that someone else had lost this dog. The animal's hostility, though, hinted at a more complicated situation. She wondered how he would react to Stefan Rigatos.

* * * * *

As sunset faded into twilight, the dog whimpered and ran downstairs to the laundry room, where he planted himself with his eyes fixed on the door to the garage. "What's wrong with you? You just went out half an hour ago." He replied with a single short bark and pawed at the doorknob. "Okay, have it your way." Vicki fastened on the leash before escorting him into the yard. She wouldn't take a chance on his leaping the fence. She faced away from him to accommodate his eccentric habits but kept the leash looped securely around her fingers.

When she led him through the garage, he lay flat in front of the inner door and refused to walk into the house. No amount of tugging could force him to his feet. "Why don't you want to come inside? Do you think I'm going to let you run around the yard by yourself where you can do your Houdini thing again? Forget it." Rather than struggle with him, she left him shut in the garage while she got ready for his alleged master's visit.

She washed up, changed into a sleeveless blouse, combed her hair and put on lipstick. Meeting her own eyes in the mirror, she asked herself why she was primping for a man she hardly knew. "I don't care what he thinks of my looks. I've had it with men, remember?" She assured herself she just wanted to look like a respectable adult, not a ditz who would keep losing somebody else's pet. The last thing she wanted was to get entangled with somebody new—not before she sorted out her feelings about the breakup. From her early teens on, she'd dealt best with males on a friendly level, especially in animal-related contexts. Phil's interest had flattered her or as she now realized, dazzled her. All the time he must have seen her, not as her true self, but as raw material to remold into the kind of woman he really wanted. *How could I have let myself get suckered in by a man who thought pets carried germs and my job was a waste of my education?*

When the doorbell rang around eight p.m. she remembered Nick's worrywart admonitions just in time to peek out the door with the chain on instead of opening it immediately. She recognized the man at once. With his glossy black hair curling down his neck and his chocolate-brown eyes, he would have been hard to forget, even if she hadn't recently conjured him in a dream. His level gaze made her face flush, as if he could read her mind or, impossibly, remember that imaginary encounter. The details she couldn't help remembering made her nipples tighten and a trickle of warmth seep between her thighs. "Come in, Mr. Rigatos." She unhooked the chain and opened the door.

"Stefan," he said. "We aren't at the clinic now. I haven't forgotten how much help you were when Caesar was sick." He clasped her hand for only a few seconds but long enough to make her pulse stutter annoyingly. She had to put that dream out of her mind or she'd never be able to carry on a conversation with the man.

"He was a fighter, wasn't he? It was sad watching him go downhill like that but he had a good long life." She remembered Stefan's distress over his cat's illness, obvious even through the stoic facade he'd projected. When the doctor had first diagnosed Caesar's kidney disease, she'd marveled at such an affluent man's attachment to a scruffy, mixed-breed tomcat. While she didn't know much about men's clothes, she could tell Stefan's didn't come off the rack at the discount store and the Lexus parked outside the vet's office had reinforced the impression. He hadn't struck her as the kind of man who would go to the expense and trouble of dialysis for a pet, not to mention accept the day-to-day mess. Lots of owners would have had the cat put down as soon as incontinence became a problem, rather than deal with stains on the carpet. Stefan, though, had postponed the euthanasia decision as long as possible, yielding to the inevitable only when the cat seemed to be suffering.

"He did," Stefan said. "Partly thanks to you. And you made that last day a little easier."

She couldn't say she'd just been doing her job, because that statement would have rung false. Giving up her break to invite him for coffee and a decompressing conversation after the cat's death had gone beyond a vet tech's normal job description. So she skipped to the purpose of this visit. "You didn't have a dog then, did you? We never saw him for a checkup." She led the way upstairs to the living room.

"No, I haven't had him very long."

"What's his name?" *I'll bet it isn't Rover.* She perched on the edge of a chair, while Stefan, at her gestured invitation, sprawled on the couch. Just as well she'd chosen not to sit on the couch. That way she couldn't be tempted to touch him.

"Sirius."

She blinked at the unusual name. Then the meaning sank in. "Oh, after the dog star."

"Right." He lounged with his arms spread over the back of the sofa, not appearing in a big rush to claim his pet.

"When did you lose him?"

"Thursday afternoon."

"Yes, that's when this dog ran into my brother's car." The coincidence that both Stefan's Saint Bernard and Ms. Morrigan's had disappeared on the same day Vicki had found "her" dog seemed less coincidental every minute. "But don't worry, it was almost stopped at the time, so he didn't get significantly hurt. He looks fine now."

"That's a relief. But, then, I know I could trust you to take excellent care of him."

The dark-chocolate smoothness of his voice, echoing its tone in her nocturnal fantasy, made her stomach flutter. Still more unsettling was the implication that he knew her better than their past meetings could justify. She stood up, wrenching her eyes away from his. "I'll go get him."

This time she took the leash, in case the animal showed unpredictable hostility again. No need to worry about that, as it happened. He'd vanished once more. The door from the garage to the backyard stood ajar, though she was sure she'd closed it firmly. Could Diana Morrigan have sneaked in and snatched him? Surely he would have barked, even attacked her. Unless the woman had baited him with drugged meat. A sour taste of anger welled in Vicki's throat at that idea.

And how could she confess to Stefan that she'd lost his pet? Bracing herself, she marched into the living room and stood in front of the couch like a prisoner before a firing squad. "I don't know how to tell you this but the dog's escaped."

Stefan said in an oddly calm tone, "He does have a talent for that."

She twisted the leash between her hands. "Well, unless he grew opposable thumbs, I don't know how he did it. I was sure I left the door shut. Unless somebody stole him. There was a woman who dropped by today."

Stefan's eyes darkened. "Who?"

"She claimed he was her dog but he couldn't stand the sight of her."

After a moment's hesitation, as if debating what to say next, he stood up. "If it was Diana Morrigan, no wonder."

"You know her?"

"We have a sort of history."

Vicki felt a twinge of irritation that surprised her. Why should she care about a relationship between Stefan and that woman? Even if Ms. Morrigan's sleek, stylish appearance made Vicki feel like an animated haystack. "Do you mean the dog belongs to both of you?"

"You might call it a custody dispute. But legally, Sirius is mine. And the way she's treated him, he has good reason to hate her."

"If he comes back, I'll chain him at night from now on. He disappeared the same way before and he showed up this morning on his own."

"He must like you," Stefan said. "Understandably." He squeezed her hand. His warm, solid grip made her insides flutter. His luscious brown eyes enhanced the effect.

"Let's look for him," she said, snatching her hand away. "If we're lucky, he ran away on his own and hasn't gone far." Not that she cherished much hope of finding Sirius. Her theory that Ms. Morrigan had abducted him seemed much more probable.

Carrying a flashlight, she prowled up and down the adjacent blocks with Stefan, both of them calling the dog's name. It felt natural to loop her arm through Stefan's for support in the dark patches between street lamps. After all, these old sidewalks had a lot of cracks and bumps.

"What made you decide to get a dog? Especially a huge hairy one like that?"

"Don't you care for size and fur?" His voice teased her at the same time his breath tickled her hair. She hoped he didn't notice the shiver that rippled through her.

"Oh, I think he's a beautiful animal. An absolute sweetheart. He's just so different from your last pet."

"That's probably why I chose him. I didn't want another cat to remind me of Caesar. I've never thanked you properly for how you took care of him. Of both of us."

She blushed, glad the dark would keep him from noticing. "I could tell he meant a lot to you."

She remembered watching Stefan gently cradle the emaciated cat when he'd brought him in, already tranquilized, for the lethal injection. She'd rested her hand on top of Stefan's as he'd held the cat still for the sodium pentobarbital IV. She'd kept her eyes on the cat instead of the man's face but the husky tone of his voice had made it clear that he was choking back tears. On impulse, since she'd been due for her lunch break anyway, she'd invited him to join her at a diner in the next block. While she'd eaten a sandwich and salad, he'd sipped coffee and reminisced about Caesar's early years as a feisty kitten and scrappy tomcat.

After half an hour of roaming from street to street, calling the dog, she had to admit how little chance they had of finding him. "I can't tell you how sorry I am about losing him. I feel terrible."

"Not your fault," Stefan said. "Not if Diana stole him."

"Well, if she didn't and he does show up on his own again, I swear I'll be more careful."

He paused in front of her house, clasping both of her hands in his. "May I come back tomorrow evening about the same time, in case he's here?"

"Sure." She silently scolded herself for the way she reacted to his casual touch, not to mention her irrational wish that he wanted to visit again for a more personal reason than searching for a lost pet. On the other hand, if he only wanted to check on Sirius, he could phone, couldn't he? Maybe that hope wasn't so irrational. *Forget that. I'm vowing celibacy, remember?*

"One more thing," he said, releasing her hands. "Sirius had a silver disk on a chain around his neck. Did you find it?"

That question settled her doubts. The animal belonged to Stefan, not Ms. Morrigan, who hadn't mentioned the necklace. "Yes. I couldn't imagine why a dog would be wearing that."

Without volunteering an answer, he said, "That's a relief. I wouldn't want to lose it. I wonder if you could give it to me now."

She took a pace backward, toward the porch steps. "I'm embarrassed to say no but I feel I have to. Sure, I'm pretty well convinced the dog belongs more to you than that woman but I don't have proof. As long as I've got any doubts, I don't think I should just hand over such a valuable piece of jewelry."

After a moment of tense silence, he let out a long breath. "Of course. I understand and I admire your principles. I'll see you tomorrow night."

She watched him drive away, annoyed with herself at the excitement that trickled through her at the thought of seeing him again.

Too agitated to sleep, she sat in the living room in her nightgown for hours, watching vintage movies on cable TV. Around midnight, she heard low-pitched barking in the backyard. Shuffling on a robe to check whether the prodigal had returned, she thought, *Tomorrow I'm getting him a chain for sure.*

* * * * *

When the man appeared beside her bed this time, she recognized him instantly. "I'm dreaming again," she said, "and I know who you are. You're Stefan Rigatos."

"Yes." His voice caressed her the way his fingers had the last time she'd dreamed of him. "Am I still welcome?"

"Sure. What could it hurt? But I don't understand why you're here."

"Does it matter?" He sat on the edge of the mattress and ran his hands from her shoulders down the front of her body to skim her thighs. "When I sleep, I reach out to you."

That remark made it sound as if he dreamed along with her. She didn't like that idea. Her dreams belonged to her. They weren't some kind of time-share. "Why me?"

He arched his eyebrows as if surprised by the question. "Because of your welcoming kindness. Also your deliciously ripe body."

Her skin quivered. "I'm not a fruit."

"Oh, no? Peaches and cream." He touched her cheek. "And cherries." His finger outlined her lips. She darted her tongue out but his hand moved too quickly for her to catch him. "Strawberries." He touched each nipple in turn, so lightly she didn't have time to react with more than a gasp of indrawn breath. With one fingertip, he traced a line from the hollow of her throat to the vee between her breasts. "Or maybe a flower opening to let me sip your nectar." He leaned over to flick his tongue along the path his finger had just followed.

A shaky giggle rippled through her. "That's so corny."

"But you do have a bud. And petals. Here." His hand brushed her pussy, a ghost of a touch that made her flesh prickle. "I can imagine you in a bower of blossoms. Would you like to join me there?"

"Yes." Her breath caught in her throat so that she could hardly speak.

Her dark bedroom dissolved into a garden dappled with sunlight sifting through the leaves of huge rosebushes. All of them hung heavy with blooms, crimson, pink and white, exuding an aroma so thick it felt almost like a honeyed liquid flowing over her naked body. She lay on the ground with Stefan reclining next to her.

He didn't have any clothes, either. She scanned his chest, sprinkled with dark hair, and the lean, tautly muscled curves and angles of his hips and legs. His cock jutted out, inviting her attention. When she ran a fingernail up the front of it, it hardened further and he gasped. The air was just warm enough to make her welcome the breeze that stirred the branches. The grass should have itched and the ground should have had at least a few uncomfortable lumps. Instead, it felt like a bed draped with velvet. "Where is here?"

"A corner of the garden at the house where I lived when I was a teenager. Or an improved version of it, actually."

"How'd you do this?" She ran a hand over the fine hairs on his chest. When she grazed a pebbled nipple, he sighed aloud.

"Lucid dreaming," he said. He cupped one of her breasts and the nipple peaked in his palm. "Most people have the ability on a latent level. They just don't know how to access it. When you master the technique, you can shape a dream into anything you want."

"So you're in charge of this dream?"

He nodded. "Is that all right with you?" He stroked the eager nipple.

She flicked one of his and smiled at the way he clasped her hand to his chest. "Yes, that's fine. Have your way with me." Her own mind had concocted this dream, so whatever he chose to do, it actually expressed her own unconscious desires. No way could the real Stefan be scripting her fantasies.

"I want to taste all of you." He nibbled each of her ears, then her neck. Again he licked the hollow at the base of her throat. She jumped at the hot, wet flicker and involuntarily dug her nails into his shoulders. "Kitten," he breathed, chilling the skin his tongue had moistened.

Shivers coursed from that spot over her body and along her arms and legs. "Keep tasting," she murmured.

"My pleasure." With his hands anchored at her hips, pinning her in place, he lapped around each breast, swirling nearer and nearer to the nipples without touching them. They prickled in the fragrant breeze. "And your pleasure, I hope. After what you've done for me, I want to give you the wildest climax you've ever had."

"Awful sure of yourself, aren't you?" Shifting restlessly with each movement of his head, she struggled to guide him to the aching peaks. "What do you mean, what I've done for you?"

"How you helped through Caesar's death, partly. As for the rest, you wouldn't believe it if I told you." His tongue flicked one nipple, then the other. The wet heat instantly changed to a tantalizing chill when the wind wafted over her.

"Keep doing that." She tried to arch her hips but he held them still.

He licked her right nipple, then the left, until her flesh threatened to transmute into molten lava. She gazed down at his head and threaded her fingers through his luxuriant pelt of black hair. Only his rapid breathing and the nudge of his erect cock against her leg reassured her that he was no less eager than she was.

The tickle in her clit begged for relief. She wiggled sideways, trying to work her pelvis under his. When he wouldn't allow that maneuver, she hooked one leg around his.

With a soft laugh, he said, "Not yet. I'm still tasting." But he did thrust his cock against her thigh before nipping a path down the front of her body. Next, his tongue traced the upper edge of her mound, just above the triangle of hair. A gush of heat flooded her slit.

She clenched her fists in the sand. "You said you wanted to sip my nectar. Do it!"

"Now?" He skimmed his fingers along the flare of her hips to the apex of the triangle, caressing the moist curls without quite touching the folds inside. Light kisses teased her inner thighs.

Her clit was twitching already. "Right now!" She opened her legs. Outside of the dream world, she would never consider begging for such treatment. She'd never felt any man's mouth there.

Flashing a feral grin, he said, "You want my tongue on your pussy?"

"Yes," she gasped.

"Then say it."

A blush scorched her skin. "I want your tongue on my pussy. Please."

Stefan's hands spread her pussy lips. The gentle wind on the damp flesh made her quiver with need. He licked her slit over and over, stopping just below the tight bud of her clit until she wanted to scream.

Finally his tongue reached the spot that craved it so urgently. The rapid butterfly flicker made her head spin. Since she couldn't hold onto him, she clutched the ground, her nails digging into the grass. Her hips arched to meet him, rose and fell in rhythm with his licking. His fast, rapid breath heated her flesh and she thrilled with the knowledge that he craved her as much as she did him. As she soared to the peak, she did scream. Tremors shuddered through her and built to an explosion, while she keened in ecstasy.

The fire between her legs still yearned to be quenched. "Come in," she whispered. "Aren't you ready?"

"What do you think?" His rigid shaft rubbed her hip. He kissed his way up her torso, with a pause at her breasts to sample her nipples again. Already she trembled on the edge of another climax. "My cock's about to burst," he said. "I've never tasted anything sweeter."

His mouth captured hers. While their tongues thrust in an impatient rhythm, he eased into her, inch by inch. She locked her legs around his hips, trying to urge him deeper. "Slowly," he whispered. "Don't want to come too fast."

"Come on, I'm ready!" She rocked under him.

He plunged in with a loud groan. Bracing himself above her, he found the angle that rubbed the base of his shaft against her clit. Combined with the penetration that made his cock head stroke the sensitive spot deep inside her, that rhythm made her sheath ripple with the onset of her release. His eyes held hers captive. "That's right. Come for me."

With an inarticulate roar, he thrust deep inside and surrendered to his own climax. She tumbled off the edge of the world with him.

All thought dissolved into a silvery mist. When Vicki opened her eyes, the dappled shadows of the rosebushes still filtered the afternoon sun. She rested in Stefan's arms, her head pillowed on his shoulder as he lay on his back. The breeze scattered a shower of petals over their nude bodies. He raised his head to blow a petal off her breast with a gentle puff of breath. A shivery laugh bubbled out of her.

"Ready to go home?" he said.

"I guess we have to sometime."

"I don't want to leave you but you need rest. I'll be back tomorrow night." His lips grazed her cheek and nibbled playfully on her earlobe. "I can hardly wait to hear you scream when you come again."

The next moment, they lay together on her bed at midnight instead of in the sunlit garden. He kissed her hair and caressed her shoulders. "One thing I've been wondering. The silver necklace you took off the dog—is it in this room?"

Chapter Five

ཀྵ

"What?" She disentangled herself from his embrace and sat up. "Why are you asking me that now?"

"Don't you want it off your hands?" He ran his fingers up her arm.

She edged away from him. "This is a fantasy, right? No mundane conversation allowed."

As soon as she made that pronouncement, the vision vanished like a bubble popping. Awake in her dark bedroom, massaging the spot between her legs that still ached, she wondered why her unconscious mind had fixated so insistently on this man.

* * * * *

Sunday morning, she phoned Stefan to report that the dog had reappeared. She reached his answering machine. The sound of his recorded voice, along with anticipation of seeing him again that evening, generated a flutter under her ribs. *Don't be an idiot,* she scolded herself. *After he gets his pet back, you'll never see him again.*

That afternoon, she went out to buy a chain and a choke collar. To her relief, when she got home she found the dog still safely confined. The second she opened the door between garage and kitchen, he trotted over to her and licked her hands.

"Yuck, dog slime!" But she couldn't help laughing at his enthusiasm. "Nice to see somebody likes me that much. Is your name Sirius, boy?"

He wagged his tail, his mouth open, panting, almost as if smiling.

She escorted him into the backyard, afraid to trust him out of her sight. After ducking behind the bushes for a minute, he charged into the middle of the yard straight for a tree. He rose onto his hind legs, planting his front paws on the trunk and barked furiously.

"What's wrong with you? Do you see a squirrel?" This frantic behavior looked so different from his usual sedate manner.

A crow swooped from a branch of the tree and dive-bombed the dog. He crouched, ears flattened and growled. When the bird circled around for another attack, Sirius jumped at it. It flew off.

"What was all that about? Come on, time to go in." She hooked her fingers around his collar and led him inside. "I have no idea why you keep running off at the same time every night or how the heck you're doing it but it's got to stop." She rattled the plastic bag containing her purchases. "From now on, you'll have to be chained when I leave. Sorry." She unwrapped the collar to try it on his neck. "Don't worry, this is a top-quality brand. It won't hurt a bit.

Sirius lay at her feet, gazing up at her with rapt attention, as if committing her words to memory. He looked disgruntled when she fitted the chain-link choke collar on him but he didn't resist.

"Okay, that should work. You don't have to wear it all the time, only when I need to put you on the chain."

He shook himself then ambled out of the kitchen. Just as she finished stashing the collar and chain in the cabinet under the sink, the dog barked from the living room. She hurried into the living room and found him on the couch staring out the window.

"Get off there right now!"

He jumped onto the floor and at the same instant, the doorbell rang.

Diana Morrigan stood on the porch. In a sleeveless aquamarine blouse and matching Capri pants, she looked cooler than she had a right to on a humid summer day. She held a leash in one hand. Sirius planted himself beside Vicki, a growl rumbling in his chest.

"Oh," she said, detesting how flustered the sight of this woman made her feel. "I wasn't expecting you." She quickly stepped onto the porch to avoid inviting the visitor inside. The dog emerged with her and sat at her left side as neatly as if performing in an obedience trial.

The blonde woman's eyes scanned up and down Vicki's body then shifted to the dog. "I was wondering whether you've made your decision about Rover. I'm very anxious to take him home." Her tone didn't convey anxiety. Rather, she sounded secretly amused and not in a kindly way.

"Sorry, I haven't decided what to do." She could have repeated the fact that another person had made a counterclaim but somehow she didn't want to mention Stefan's visit to Ms. Morrigan. *Because I don't want to get in the crossfire of a nasty breakup, if that's what it is.*

The woman's eyes narrowed. "You should decide now. You want to get that beast off your hands." She began twisting the leash, looping it in the middle and braiding the two lengths together, just as she had on her earlier visit. Sirius emitted an almost subsonic growl.

"No, I'm in no hurry for that. I enjoy having him around. He's very sweet."

"Sweet?" Ms. Morrigan smirked. "You haven't known him long." She hummed, still weaving the halves of the leash.

The tuneless hum seemed to insinuate itself into Vicki's brain. It buzzed around inside her skull like a wasp in a jar. Her vision grayed. *There she goes again, trying to hypnotize me.*

Vicki knew she should fight, but she couldn't summon the will.

Something bumped into her leg. The dog. Her knees wobbled. She rested her hand on his back for support. The humming grew louder. Black spots swarmed in front of her eyes. The floor floated up to meet her.

A fusillade of barking jolted her to consciousness. She lay flat on her back on the porch. The dog, alternately barking and snarling, crouched between her and Ms. Morrigan. His lips curled back, exposing a muzzle full of fangs.

The blonde woman edged down the steps to the sidewalk. Scrambling to her feet, Vicki retreated toward the door.

"Have it your way. Later you'll regret not giving him up when I asked nicely." Ms. Morrigan whirled around and marched to her car.

The dog barked after her, his fur bristling. Shaking, Vicki stood with one hand on the doorknob. *Maybe she's right about one thing. Maybe he isn't as gentle as he looks.*

When the woman's car disappeared around the corner, he emitted one final snarl and turned toward Vicki. She pushed the door ajar, prepared to duck inside and slam it if he made a hostile move. The hair on his back flattened and his tail drooped. He wagged it tentatively and slinked toward her.

"Sirius?"

He nosed her hand and panted as if he'd never attacked anyone in his life. "Are you sure I can trust you?" He whined and licked her fingers. "I've seen enough friendly-looking animals turn on people unpredictably. I should take you to the SPCA right now."

Ears perked forward, he whined again and rubbed his head against her hip like a giant cat. "I guess I'm a total pushover." She scratched behind his ears. His tongue lolled from his gaping mouth and his tail wagged faster. "Wish I knew what she's done that makes you hate her so much."

He yipped softly as if trying to answer. When Vicki opened the door farther, he shoved past her into the house. "Don't worry," she said. "I won't turn you over to that rhymes-with-witch if I can possibly avoid it."

* * * * *

That evening at dusk, Sirius once again insisted on going outside. Because he wouldn't come in even when she tried to drag him, she chained him next to the door between garage and backyard, with bowls of food and water. He accepted the restraint with suspicious docility. "I hope you don't think you can wiggle out of this, even if you are a canine Houdini."

About the time she expected Stefan, though, she checked on the dog and found the collar lying on the ground at the end of the chain, empty. "I've had it with this crazy routine!" she yelled into the night. "Sirius, where the heck are you?"

No answer, of course. The dog wouldn't be roaming the streets waiting for her to call him. This time, some human agent must have spirited him away.

Before she could go into the house, she heard a car engine. Hurrying around front, she found Stefan's sports car pulling into the driveway behind her economy compact.

She stormed up to confront him the moment he opened his door. "Okay, what kind of game are you playing?"

He held up both hands in mock surrender. "Whoa, I plead innocent, whatever it is. What are you talking about?"

She glared at him with her hands on her hips. "The dog vanished again."

"From which you conclude what?" He stepped out of the car and stared down at her, almost close enough for her to feel his breath.

She told herself her heart was racing purely from exasperation. "That animal couldn't have slipped off a choke chain with his paws. Did you sneak him out of my yard?"

"Now, if I'd done that, why would I bother to show up?"

With a sigh, she said, "You've got me there. If you didn't do it, that woman, Diana Morrigan, must have stolen him."

"Paws or not, he's an unusually clever animal. Let's not jump to conclusions."

"Come on, you're not seriously suggesting he escaped on his own. If it wasn't her, some neighbor must be playing tricks on me, which makes no sense at all." Unless it was Phil. No, from what she'd observed of the dog's behavior so far, he had better sense than to go off tamely with a jerk like Phil.

"Don't get upset, I'm sure he'll be all right." Stefan cupped the side of her head briefly, his thumb grazing her cheek.

Molten heat poured through her. She flushed, thankful that he couldn't know about her dreams. Remembering them made it almost impossible to meet his eyes. She flinched away from his touch.

"Let's have another try at looking for the prodigal canine." Just as he had the night before, Stefan sounded remarkably nonchalant about his pet's absence.

"Sure, why not?" She got the flashlight from the kitchen and they strolled along the sidewalk together, calling the dog's name. "I feel like a fool, scouring the neighborhood for an animal that couldn't possibly have run away by himself."

"It's not totally impossible. If he got some slack into the collar, he could have pawed it over his head."

"Except no dog would have the intelligence not to pull it tight trying to escape. Granted, he's smart. He looks at me when I'm talking like he understands every word. But he couldn't be that smart."

"He does understand a lot of words. Animals have more brains than we give them credit for." By now they'd covered half a mile from Vicki's house. Stefan nodded toward the dark mass of trees behind her street. "What's over there?"

"The Back Creek Nature Park. It has trails, a lagoon, a nature center building—stuff like that. If he did run away, not that I believe it for a minute, he might have gone into the woods there."

"Let's take a look." He plucked the flashlight from her hand and strode toward the trees.

"If you want to spend the time on a wild goose chase, it's okay with me." Maybe he was inventing an excuse to hang around with her a while longer, a notion that pleased her more than it should have.

When they stepped onto the trail leading into the park, he switched on the flashlight and clasped her right hand in his left. A patch of warmth expanded just below her rib cage. "If we do find Sirius," she said, "I admit, I'll miss him when he goes home."

"I'm surprised you don't have a pet," he said, aiming the light to skitter over the trail and the underbrush beside it. The loam showed no sign of paw prints. "You have such a great way with animals."

"My ex claimed he was allergic. I'm thinking of getting a cat now that we've broken up."

"Cats are more self-sufficient than dogs. You've heard the saying 'dogs have owners, cats have staff'?"

She laughed. "Sure."

"I like that about them. They'll grant affection but on their own terms. When my aunt got Caesar for me, I thought he was the only creature who understood me. You know how adolescents are and I was more of an introverted loner than most."

She could imagine him at that age, cultivating catlike aloofness. "You had him that long? Wow."

"I lived with my Aunt Irene. We got along okay most of the time, even if she didn't seem to know what to do with a teenage boy. One of the few fights we had happened when she released my tarantulas into the wild."

An involuntary "Eeuw" escaped from Vicki. She stumbled and he tightened his grip to support her. "Your what?"

"Don't knock it. They make very entertaining pets. One of them escaped from the terrarium and Aunt Irene blew her top. The worst of it was, I'd paid for the spiders and their paraphernalia with my own money. After I'd sulked for three days, she admitted she'd overreacted." Vicki heard a smile in his voice. "We reached a negotiated settlement. No more pets with more or fewer than four legs. She got Caesar for me. She named him that because she taught high-school Latin."

"Oh, I wondered why such a nonaristocratic animal was named after an emperor."

"He wasn't always as scruffy-looking as when you first saw him. The kidney failure was already affecting his coat quality by then."

"I know how it feels to lose an old pet. I went through the same thing almost a year ago." She told him about her elderly Border Collie that had died. "I inherited him from my parents, so it hurt even more. Like you and your aunt, I guess. None of my business but what happened to your folks?"

"I don't mind talking about it. My father was an officer in the Navy. When I was pretty young, Mom got sick of that lifestyle—moving around all the time—and ran off with another man. He didn't want a kid in the picture." The hint of bitterness in Stefan's tone belied his statement that the topic didn't bother him.

"That must have been rough." She could hardly resist the impulse to offer him a comforting touch. She had to keep reminding herself that the dream intimacy had happened only in her mind. In real life they barely knew each other.

He shrugged. "It was a long time ago. I stayed with Aunt Irene whenever Dad was on sea duty, which meant about two years out of every four. Looking back, I realize he must have been under heavy stress. He died of a heart attack when I was thirteen, so after that I lived with my aunt full-time."

Because it would have felt intrusive to express sympathy again, she simply asked, "No other relatives?"

"Dad's parents were Greek immigrants. They had him late in life, so they were too old by then to handle a kid." His tone softened. "They deserved a rest. They owned a restaurant most of their lives. Too bad most married people don't have the kind of life together they had."

Vicki came to an abrupt stop and tried to scan his face in the dark. "What makes you think most of them don't?"

"Do you think so?" His voice took on a brittle edge.

"Sure, my parents did."

"They belonged to an older generation. I haven't seen that kind of relationship between any couples our age."

"Then maybe you run in the wrong circles." She pulled her hand out of his and walked briskly along the trail, glancing from side to side in search of dog footprints.

"I'd like to believe that," he said. "But I'm too realistic."

The tinge of wistfulness in that remark almost banished her annoyance at him but not quite. "Sounds more like another kind of delusion to me," she muttered. As if she had any right to an opinion, come to think of it, considering the bad judgment she'd used with Phil.

She picked up her pace, trying to outrun her thoughts. At a bend in the path, she snagged her foot on a tree root. With a gasp, she tripped. Stefan caught her elbow and steadied her. She automatically clutched his arm. Without thinking, she let her hand slide from there to his chest, where it came to rest against his breastbone.

"Not so fast." His chest vibrated with amusement under her open palm. The sensation reminded her of that uncannily realistic dream. "You'll never find the dog by racing along in the dark that way."

"We'll never find him out here anyhow, even if that woman didn't snatch him." She edged away from Stefan and swept her hair back from her damp forehead in a gesture of exasperation. "This was a silly idea. Let's go back."

"I'll get in touch with Diana tomorrow and try to find out whether she did take Sirius. Not that I'm sure she would admit it."

Back at the house, when Vicki walked with Stefan around front to his car, she noticed a crow perched in the tree nearest the porch. "That's funny, I didn't think crows were nocturnal."

Stefan waved and shouted at the bird, "Go away, beat it!" The black shape, even larger than most of its kind, only flapped its wings and cawed as if in derision. He picked up a rock and threw it into the tree. With another caw, the bird launched itself into the air and flew out of sight.

Vicki felt she should object to his flinging rocks around so close to her windows but she was glad to see the creature gone. "Weird," she said. "I wonder if that's the same crow the dog was barking at today."

"He must have been trying to protect you."

She laughed. "Against a crow?"

"It's not natural for a bird to hang around like that, unless it's after food or something. Maybe it's rabid."

"Birds don't get rabies, only mammals."

"Well, I'll defer to your professional expertise on that point." He captured her hand in both of his. When she caught herself gazing up into his eyes, she retreated onto the porch steps, trying to equalize their heights. "I'd like to see you again. Do I have to use Sirius as an excuse?"

She swallowed. "Is that what you've been doing?" She hoped her voice didn't quiver.

"Partly. Of course I want my dog back. But I also want to take you out. How about tomorrow night?" After a few seconds hesitation, he added, "Unless you're involved with someone?"

"No. I was but I broke up with him a few days ago. Definitely all over."

"Great." A smile of undisguised pleasure lit up his face. "Then how about dinner?"

I shouldn't. He's a man, same gender as Phil. The half of the human species I'm supposed to keep my distance from, remember? So where did the words that leaped out of her mouth come from? The words, "I'd love to."

* * * * *

It didn't surprise her to open her eyes and find Stefan, naked again, standing over her in the moonlight that poured through her window. *Was there a full moon tonight? Doesn't matter, anything can happen in a dream.* "You're back. Why?"

"Do you have to ask? Because you have what I need. Because I want to come inside you again."

To fend off the impulse to rub against him like a cat, she opted for a flippant retort. "What's with the subtlety? Say what you really think."

"I enjoyed our walk in the woods so much I couldn't wait for our dinner appointment." He touched the valley between her breasts and her nightgown evaporated like mist. "I want to taste your passion in real life."

Sitting up, she bent her knees and wrapped her arms around them. "Not going to happen. Dream sex is all you get."

He laughed softly. "You don't object to that?" He sat beside her and planted a kiss on her shoulder.

"No, it's nice and safe." A dream man couldn't wreck her life.

"You have a strange idea of safety." He leaned across her to kiss the other shoulder. She sighed and threw her head back, silently inviting him to nuzzle her throat. He accepted the invitation.

"Mmm. You're the best fantasy lover I've ever had." She didn't think it necessary to add that he was the only one.

"Thanks…I think," he said with a wry smile before bending to kiss her shoulder.

His breath raised goose bumps all over her body. "I can't believe how real this feels."

He shrugged. "That's how lucid dreaming works. Shall I demonstrate my talents by taking you somewhere else?"

She tangled her fingers in his hair and trembled at the flicker of his tongue on the delicate skin of her throat. "How about a beach?"

Immediately, she found herself lying on sand under a palm tree. Waves breaking on a rocky shoreline glistened in the light of a full moon. More stars than she'd ever seen before sparkled with unnatural brightness. Not only that, the rocks themselves emitted a silvery glow. The same aura outlined Stefan's body as he knelt beside her. "There's no beach like this around here."

"You didn't specify a location."

Laughing, she reached for him. He stretched on top of her, cradled between her open thighs. The tangy scent of salt air tickled her nose, along with his musk and spicy aftershave. She rubbed against the slight roughness of his cheek and inhaled his essence. The sand, instead of irritating her bare back, felt like cool silk. *How did my subconscious come up with all these details?*

She ran her fingers through the wavy pelt of his hair. His mouth explored her lips, neck and shoulders, sending tiny sparks through her. To her surprise, she could actually see those sparks dancing over her skin as well as his, like static electricity in a dark room. "What's that?" she murmured. "Like fireflies?"

"Magic." He lapped the hollow between her breasts.

"Yeah, right." She sighed and arched her hips to wedge his hard cock more firmly against her pussy. His teeth gently nipped the curve of her left breast. A shock zapped straight to her clit. "On second thought, it does feel pretty magical."

She bit his shoulder in retaliation. He buried his face in her neck and growled, the rumble in his chest making her insides vibrate. She skimmed her nails down his back over and over, in long sweeping strokes, while he nibbled her neck, shoulders and breasts. Her nipples peaked, waiting for the contact he kept denying them. She squirmed under him, the motion tantalizing her clit with the shifting pressure of his cock.

"Tell me what you want," he said, both hands caressing the swell of her hips.

"It's my dream, so you're supposed to know."

A soft laugh tickled the vee between her breasts. "It's my dream too and I want to hear you say it."

"Lick me. Here." She arched her back. "My nipples." Her hands migrated from his back to his chest, her fingers seeking the pebbled tips of his nipples.

With a gasp, he lapped one of hers.

"Oh, yeah," she sighed. "You like being touched there too?"

"Maybe not as much as you do but it feels great anyway." He ran his tongue over her other nipple and smiled at her whimper of pleasure.

Phil would never have admitted liking such a thing, even if he'd cared to spend this much time fooling around before the main event. *Forget about Phil.* In Vicki's fantasy world, he didn't exist. She tickled Stefan's nipples again, just to hear him growl like a hungry wolf. "More licking!" She laced her fingers around his head to draw his mouth down to her breasts.

His tongue shot heat through her veins to melt her core. Liquid pooled between her legs. She slithered down his body, silently begging for his erection to rub against her pussy. He did just that, while curling over her to flick his tongue across her nipples. Through the swirling fog of desire, she wondered whether his spine could possibly be that supple in real life. *I'll never find out. Don't think about reality.*

He slid up and down between her folds, spreading the juices from her slit to the taut bud above it. Like silk over steel, his cock stroked her in a long, slow rhythm. She stared into his eyes, which glowed like burning coals, brighter with every second, as if they reflected his mounting excitement. He breathed huskily, his lips parted. She locked her legs around him and threw her head back, dizzy with the thrill of his tongue on her nipples, his shaft gliding over her wet heat. Trembling on the edge, she clung to him and cried out his name.

"Come for me!" He pressed his cock head against her clit.

The pulsations began at that spot and radiated through her entire body. The sparks of light around Stefan danced before her eyes like a fountain of fireworks.

"I need to come inside you." His teeth clamped onto her shoulder. "Right now!"

The sting of the bite, not quite pain, spurred her to a fresh frenzy of excitement. Her pussy still throbbed. "Yes!" She drew him in. He arched above her. She watched the muscles of his chest and shoulders flex with each surge of his hips.

His thrusts sparked another explosion inside her. He plunged into her faster and harder as her channel rippled with aftershocks.

"Again!" he cried. The firefly lights swirled around them. A third convulsion seized her. She felt him quaking with the same tremors.

He braced himself above her, lodged to the hilt in her depths. She arched her hips to press her clit hard against him. With her legs clamped around his waist, she abandoned herself to the contractions rippling through her pussy, the pulsations of his cock echoing them. When the last shudders died away, he lay on her, his head on her shoulder. With a long sigh, she unwrapped her legs from around him and stretched them out, his cock still cradled between her thighs.

For a minute they both trembled, their breath coming in synchronized pants. Recovering, he whispered, "You see? That's what I needed from you." He kissed her cheek and her forehead. "I wish I could stop time and keep you here forever."

"Sounds like a plan." She massaged the warm, solid muscles of his shoulders. "If you can conjure up imaginary food and drinks. Or maybe we don't have to eat, since it's a dream."

He sighed. "But we do have to wake up." He lifted his head and gazed into her eyes. "Not right away, though."

"Then let's go swimming." Another thing she'd never done in her waking hours—splash in the ocean at night. "We can't drown, right? Or even catch a chill." Come to think of it, she didn't have sand sticking to her skin, either.

He leaped up. "Race you to the water!"

They ran, their bare feet kicking up showers of sand. She sloshed into the waves a couple of strides ahead of him. "You let me win."

"Merely being gallant, my fair lady."

Laughing, she splashed water in his face. When he retaliated, the salt didn't sting her eyes. He dove into the surf and she followed. The temperature felt just barely cooler than her skin. "This is great." Lifting her feet from the ocean floor, she leaned back to float. In real life she couldn't do that without floundering.

With the water up to his hips, Stefan glided in between her splayed legs. He rested his hands lightly on her waist, his thumbs caressing her. "You look beautiful with your hair streaming behind you like a mermaid."

"Now I know I'm dreaming, because I'd flunk mermaid class for sure. I can hardly dog paddle from one side of a pool to the other." Something cool and damp nudged her arm. She yelped and turned toward the source of the sensation.

A whiskery muzzle attached to a sleek head faced her. "Good grief, what's that, a seal?"

"Sea otter," Stefan said. He patted the animal. "Ozzie. He's a toy I had when I was little. My mother bought him for me at the zoo. That was before she left, of course."

A beach ball appeared out of nowhere. Stefan tossed the ball for the otter to chase. The animal caught it on his nose and bounced it back. "You try." Stefan handed her the toy.

Laughing, she batted it back and forth to the otter a few times. Ozzie barked a farewell and dove underwater. Stefan clasped her around the waist and rubbed his shaft up and down the cleft of her bottom. The water buoyed her up so that she floated in front of him, the head of his penis tantalizing her with random touches. He cupped her breasts and teased her nipples to attention.

"I need to get inside your pussy," he said, the husky timbre of his voice making his chest rumble against her back. "I need to come again."

"Already?"

He laughed. "In a dream world I can come as often as you can. Are you saying you're not ready?" One hand roamed from her breast to her slit, which responded with a rush of heat.

"Oh, yes, my pussy's ready too." She flushed at the thought of using that language to his face. But in this setting she could say anything.

He eased into her. With his arms hooked under her thighs, he strode through the water to the shallows. Stimulating her with short, brisk thrusts, he lowered both of them to their knees in the surf. Wavelets lapped her like a hundred tongues. Ripples coursed through her. With her thighs braced on either side of his, she let the rise and fall of the water set the pace of her riding the surge of his cock.

She clutched his shoulders while his thrusts quickened. The waves inside her expanded in ever-widening circles until they drowned her consciousness in ecstasy.

Still shaking, she whimpered in protest when he pulled out of her. "It's okay," he whispered, his breath warming her neck. His hands swirled over her breasts and stomach while he shifted position to kneel behind her. "Open your legs wider." He cupped her mound and spread her pussy lips, his long fingers stroking her clit.

His cock slid into her again. On his knees, he rocked back to sit with her on his lap. One hand wandered over her breasts and circled her taut nipples while the other continued to tease her clit. Her breath caught in her throat as her inner muscles tightened and quivered with the onset of another climax. She leaned back against the solid wall of his chest and reached behind her to dig her nails into his hips. With one arm he held her close while her orgasm flooded over her.

Joining her, he plunged into her depths and shot molten heat that triggered another delirious convulsion.

In the final seconds of their shared release, they drifted free of the sand and floated on the surf. The waves rocked them. Vicki luxuriated in the sensation and had no trouble breathing even with her face in the blood-warm water. A maelstrom caught them and whirled them around. They floated upward into the star-spangled sky.

Wrapped in his embrace, she stood in the middle of her bedroom. His hands stroked her flanks as if soothing a skittish pet. "Do you trust me?" he asked. His serious tone jarred against the sensual delight they'd shared.

"Did I ever say I didn't?" She tilted her head to scan his face. "Why do you ask?"

"Would you let me make love to you while you're awake?"

"I'm not sure." The reminder of mundane life was an unwelcome letdown. "I'd have to think about it, get to know you better."

"I want to be with you that way, feel your body against mine. I don't want to be limited to dreams forever." He stroked her hair. "But before we can be free to be together, I need your help. Show me where the amulet is."

Retreating a step away from him, she said, "The what?"

"The silver necklace."

"That again? Why do you keep harping on it?"

"Because I need it. I'm lost without it."

Vicki shook her head. "This is not part of my fantasy."

"Listen to me." He grabbed her shoulders. "Diana's after it too. If she gets it, she'll use it to hurt me and maybe you as well."

"Why would she want to hurt me? Somebody she doesn't even know?"

"Because you helped me."

Why did he have to spoil an erotic dream by trying to scare her? Or, more accurately, why did her subconscious add this unpleasant wrinkle to the fantasy? "You keep saying that. How have I helped you?"

"By sheltering me when I was lost. I can't explain it. You'll think I'm insane."

"Oh, as opposed to the insanity of arguing with a figment of my lust-crazed imagination?" She snatched a robe from the bedpost to shield her nude body. "If that's all you have to say, get out of here."

Chapter Six

ꟃ

Again, she woke instantly, as if her words of rejection had exorcised him. Crumpling the hem of the sheet in her fists, she wondered why her unconscious mind had concocted that argument. Maybe it symbolized her suppressed guilt over holding on to Stefan's property. Or maybe she projected her anxiety about losing his dog onto the necklace. *Thank you, Ms. Freud.* She laughed and rolled over to settle back to sleep.

* * * * *

Next morning she again woke to low-pitched barking. When she went out through the garage and opened the door to the backyard, she found the dog waiting there.

"You're purposely trying to drive me crazy, aren't you? Get in here, you hairy delinquent." She ran her fingers over the dense fur on his back.

A growl rumbled through him. He spun around and stared upward. Following the direction of his eyes, Vicki noticed another crow, or maybe the same one, perched on a nearby branch. The bird dive-bombed Sirius, who sprang onto his rear legs and snapped at it with a snarl. Again, as the crow flapped away, its squawk reminded her of a mocking laugh.

The dog trotted to the door, his plumed tail wagging as if in satisfaction at driving off his nemesis. "What are you trying to tell me? You don't like birds?"

After getting dressed and feeding and walking the dog, she herded him into the laundry room off the kitchen. "If you don't want to end up at the animal shelter, you better quit running away." Not that she would do such a thing if she could possibly help it but the dog couldn't figure that out, could he? *Good grief, I'm thinking like he can understand what I'm saying.* "Can I trust you alone in the house while I'm gone?" He sat at her feet, gazing up at her, his tail thumping. Shaking her head, she gave him a last pat, shut him in and left for work.

About ten a.m., while she was staffing the reception counter at the vet's office, Phil strolled in.

She scanned his muscular build, honed by hours at the health club, and his green eyes and sun-burnished blond hair, which had turned her to mush when they'd first met, with a total lack of interest. *Yay, I'm cured.* "What are you doing here?"

He put on a hurt expression that affected her like fingernails on a chalkboard. "No need to be rude. The way you ran out on the spur of the moment, we never got a chance to talk things over."

"I don't have anything to say to you. Have you gotten a pet since Friday?"

"What? Of course not." If anything could have increased her annoyance with him, the tinge of distaste in his brusque retort would've done it.

"I didn't think so, because you don't like animals. That should've been my first clue that we didn't belong together. So you have no reason to be here. Go away."

"Come on, Vicki, be reasonable." He leaned on the counter, practically breathing in her face.

At that moment, Dr. Brodie stepped into the waiting room and saved her from having to yell at Phil where everybody in the office could hear.

"Excuse me, did you want to make an appointment?" the doctor asked. When Phil shook his head, his face reddening, Dr. Brodie said, "Then I'll have to ask you to leave. I don't want my staff distracted from their duties."

Phil cast an appealing look at Vicki. Unable to suppress a smirk, she said, "You heard the doc."

He stalked out, letting the door bang behind him.

She bowed her head on her hands and groaned. She felt her cheeks turning pink with mortification. "Aargh. I'm so sorry. I didn't encourage him, honest."

"Don't worry about it," the doctor said. He patted her shoulder. "But have you thought about getting a restraining order?"

"Oh, no reason for that. I'm sure he won't bother you again. He's not stupid, just a jerk."

"It's you I'm concerned about. I wouldn't like to think of him harassing you at home this way."

"No, no, he's harmless." She waved her hands as if shooing flies, wishing she could whisk Phil out of her life the same way. "I just want to forget about him."

* * * * *

In dog form, Stefan prowled the windowless laundry room. Vicki had come home on her lunch hour to exercise him then had shut him in here again. He'd pawed at the knob of the kitchen door a dozen times but hadn't succeeded in turning it. He hadn't even bothered trying the door to the garage, since it was locked. So he prowled. Not that he could do much of that in a space about six by six feet, half of it occupied by the washer and dryer. He paced in tight circles, growling to himself. Aside from a bowl of fresh water, the cubicle held nothing in terms of entertainment except the appliances, a few shelves of cleaning supplies and the aroma of detergent. He'd had a sneezing fit before he'd become used to the smell. Grateful that he retained his human mind in this form, he'd already read the labels on all the boxes and bottles he could see from floor level, far from riveting material. He was tempted to knock down a few of them and scatter their contents, just to pay her back for imprisoning him in this stupefyingly dull environment.

He shook himself, scattering loose fur. No, she didn't deserve that kind of behavior, when she was only trying to keep him safe. Too bad she'd had to go back to work so soon. He already missed her, no matter how humiliating it was to be "walked". If only she'd at least put him in the kitchen. If he weren't locked in here, he could use the afternoon to search for his amulet. Although he'd tried planting his butt on the floor and refusing to enter the tiny room, her outspoken distress had broken his resolve. Vicki had obviously been prepared to stay home until she had him safely confined, even if it had taken all afternoon.

He growled again and nosed the bone-shaped chew toy she'd left him into a corner. How long could he continue the Houdini act before she found a way to keep him from escaping or, worse, gave up and consigned him to the animal shelter? Maybe he shouldn't return at midnight this time. But as a dog, where else could he go? Hiding in the woods for eighteen hours out of twenty-four didn't appeal to him. *Besides, I'd miss her. Damn.* If the dog vanished permanently, Stefan would no longer have an excuse to visit in human form. Even though she'd admitted to him what "Sirius" already knew, that she was available, he couldn't count on one date to make her eager to see him again. Not even after a series of passionate dreams to soften her up. And he did want to see her as often as possible, so much that he'd settle for doing so in the role of her temporary pet. Flinging himself full length on the beach towel she'd spread on the floor, he grudgingly admitted to himself that he accepted this role for more than the shelter and convenience it provided. He craved her nearness, her touch. More than that, he yearned to plunge into her sweet depths in the flesh, not only in dreams. To his dismay, the line he'd fed her in that last fantasy about wanting to be with her, was coming true.

Stop thinking about that, he growled to himself. *Think about persuading her to give you the amulet.* So far, he'd spent more energy seducing than interrogating.

Maybe he'd channeled a bit too much energy into the magic when he'd cast that refuge-seeking spell? It seemed to act like a magnetic field drawing him to Vicki. If he were smart, he would tear himself from her and stay as far away as possible until the effect wore off. *If I were as smart as I thought I was, I wouldn't be stuck in this predicament to begin with, would I?* At the very least, though, he should spend part of the early evening in the nature preserve, so she wouldn't directly connect the dog's disappearance with Stefan's arrival. This time he would have to make a point of slipping out before nightfall, before she thought of confining him, maybe keeping him directly under her eyes.

His ears perked up. Footsteps on the front porch. Not Vicki's. He sat up, listening for the knock he expected to hear next.

Instead, a female voice muttered words from an arcane language. *Diana!* She'd cast an unlocking spell. The door swung open with a squeak of hinges. Her soft footfalls crossed the living room carpet. "Stefan, where are you? I know you're in here."

His lips involuntarily curled back from his muzzle in a silent snarl. *Get a grip! I'm human inside, so act like it.*

"Here, boy. Come on, good doggie." Her singsong tone made his teeth hurt. After a circuit of the dining room, she strode into the kitchen. "Here, Rover, nice puppy. You're close. I can feel you. Come out, come out, wherever you are."

Her heels clicked on the linoleum. He heard her breathing as she paused outside the closed laundry room door. The fragrance of her perfume drifted to his nose. "Hmm, I wonder." She opened the door a crack.

With a roar of fury, he lunged at it. She slammed it shut just in time.

"Tsk, tsk. Naughty pup. I'll be back to deal with you in a minute. I have another job first."

Her retreating footsteps headed upstairs. Overhead, she explored the bedrooms until she came to what he identified by its position as Vicki's. A drawer opened and closed. Was Diana searching for the amulet? He braced himself for her alien touch upon that highly personal item. Instead of rummaging through other drawers, though, she marched downstairs immediately.

What was that about? Seconds later, she stood outside the laundry room again. "Stefan? Why don't you come with me and save both of us a lot of trouble?"

He defied her with a gruff bark.

"Now, don't be that way." She chanted a spell. Its energy seeped under the door and enveloped him like a Chanel-scented fog. It snaked around his neck like a vine and tugged him toward the door. Compulsion magic to force him to follow her.

He braced all four legs and shook it off, splashing it away from him like water.

"Don't fight me, Stefan. Yield and come home with me. If not, I'll make it even worse for you when I finally get you in my power."

Though he wanted to laugh at her gloating like a cartoon villainess, he felt the pressure of her magic winding around his neck, choking him. He summoned his own power and expelled it with all the force he had left. His shield settled over him like a familiar cloak.

Her anger scorched the air. "So that last-minute spell you cast on yourself guarded you from my power. That explains why you aren't a dog twenty-four hours a day. You activated that amulet you were wearing, didn't you?" She paused as if expecting a reply. He didn't move. "Don't count on that shield to protect you forever. If I can catch you weakened somehow, I know I can break through it. Meanwhile, wait until you see what I do to that new woman of yours."

Rage boiled up in his chest. He flung himself at the door with an outburst of barking and growling. Diana laughed softly and turned away.

When his fury died down, he sensed she was gone. He collapsed, panting. What had she meant by that taunt? Bad enough that she was using the crow to spy on this house through its eyes. Stefan knew if Diana launched a direct attack, he couldn't hope to protect Vicki every minute. The thought of her becoming an innocent victim of Diana's wrath made his stomach churn. *Vicki is mine! I won't let her get hurt.* Replaying his own thought, he yelped in shock. *Mine?* What was happening to him?

* * * * *

When Vicki got home and unlocked the door from the garage into the laundry room, the dog bumped against her, wagging his entire rear half and shoving his nose into her hands. She laughed. "Okay, I'm glad to see you too." Leashing him, she walked him into the yard. "I don't care whether you like it or not. You don't get to run loose anymore. How would I explain it to Stefan if you got hit by a car the next time you pulled that vanishing act?"

Speaking the man's name aloud made her skin tingle with anticipation. This evening they'd have their first real date. Her cheeks grew hot with the memory of those sizzling dreams. How could she face him with those images in her head?

Just as she brought Sirius inside, the phone rang. Before picking it up, she waited for a message on the answering machine rather than chance a verbal clash with Phil. Her brother Nick's voice followed the beep.

She picked up in mid-sentence. "Hi, what's happening?"

"Nothing with me," Nick said. "I'm just calling to check on you. Phil phoned me this afternoon, trying to recruit me to 'talk some sense' into you. Between us guys—help him handle the irrational female. I told him to drop dead."

She giggled. "Really?"

"Well, no, I put it more politely. We lawyers are trained in diplomatic euphemisms, you know."

"Too bad. So what are you calling for?"

"Just wondered if you'd had any trouble with him."

"Well..." She didn't want to stir Nick's protective instincts by admitting what had happened that day. On the other hand, he would sense any evasion and worm the story out of her anyhow. "He did drop in at the clinic this morning. No big deal."

"Harassment at the workplace?" As she'd expected, Nick sounded more worried than the situation justified. "Have you thought about getting a restraining order?"

"You sound like Dr. Brodie but he has the excuse of being old enough to be my father."

"Don't make light of the problem. You mentioned Phil owns a gun."

She snorted. "Come on, can you actually imagine him shooting me?"

After placating Nick, she fed the dog, showered and dressed for dinner. Because Stefan hadn't mentioned where he planned to take her, she compromised on a casual skirt and blouse with sandals. By then, she still had plenty of time before he was due. "What am I thinking, getting ready early?" she said to the dog with a pat on his massive head. "The reputation of women everywhere will never recover."

Too restless to hang around the house, she consigned the dog to the laundry room again and drove to the liquor store for a bottle of white wine to serve when Stefan arrived to pick her up. A quick half glass for each of them would set the scene for a relaxing social evening, as opposed to a dog-hunting expedition.

When she pulled into her driveway twenty minutes later, she found a familiar midnight blue, four-door sedan at the curb. *Oh, damn, it's Phil again.* She marched over to the car but he wasn't in the driver's seat. Fuming, she strode up the porch steps, a paper bag in one arm and her purse swinging from her shoulder.

A figure stepped from the corner of the porch and a hand clamped onto her wrist. She let out an involuntary shriek. From inside the house, Sirius answered her with a gruff bark.

Phil placed the forefinger of his other hand on her lips. "Take it easy. It's just me."

She glared at him and tried to wrench her arm out of his grip. He didn't release her. "Let go of me, you idiot." Though her heart still raced from the shock of being grabbed, she refused to act afraid of the man she'd dated for two years.

"I'll do that after you hear me out." He plucked the bag from her and set it on a lawn chair by the front door. "I see you still have that thing." He waved at the giant inflatable crab. "Are you sure it's not lonely? Maybe you should get a flock of plastic flamingos and a dozen garden gnomes too."

She sighed. "I'm busy, Phil. What do you want?"

"Why won't you at least talk to me? You didn't even give me the courtesy of saying goodbye to my face. Is that fair?"

"Well..." She ground her teeth in annoyance. For a second he'd actually gotten to her with that self-pitying line. "Don't try to guilt me into changing my mind. We had plenty of conversations about what you wanted out of me. They never went anywhere."

In the background, the dog barked so loudly she wondered why the windows didn't rattle.

"What the hell is that?"

"A dog I'm watching for a friend." She didn't want to go into the details with Phil and start an irrelevant argument.

He cast a nervous glance toward that side of the house. "Then we'd better talk in my car."

"What part of 'I have nothing to say to you' do you not understand?"

"Listen, honey," he said with a show of exaggerated patience, "just one conversation and after that, if you still want me out of your life, I promise I'll leave you alone."

Again she tried to tug her wrist out of his grasp but he didn't let go. "Oh, all right." She plopped her purse on the chair with the wine bag and folded her arms. "So talk. And make it fast."

"In the car."

"Forget that!"

His expression of long-suffering patience shifted to a scowl. "I said I want you in the car." He grabbed her arm and pulled.

When she tugged in the opposite direction, he retaliated with a hard jerk. She had to let him haul her down the steps to avoid falling down them. He pulled her toward the curb.

"Have you gone crazy? Let go." Struggling against his grip, she glanced around at the nearest yards. No neighbors in sight. Her heartbeat speeded up and her mouth went dry.

Phil gave her a teeth-rattling shake, opened the car door and shoved her toward the back seat of his car. Before she could recover from the shock, he pushed her in and slammed the door.

Instead of joining her in the back, he slipped into the driver's seat. She realized what he had in mind only when the childproof locks clicked into place. "Hey, what do you think you're doing?"

"Taking you to my place for a little privacy. Don't worry, I won't hurt you. You know that, don't you?"

"I don't know anything except that you've completely lost your mind! Let me out of here!" She rattled the door handle and banged on the window with her palms. It took only a few seconds for her to realize how useless that gesture was, with nobody around to notice the commotion.

Except Sirius, whom she could still hear barking as if he too, had gone insane.

* * * * *

Hours seemed to drag past before Stefan felt the surge of magic that transformed him back into a man, though he knew less than half an hour had lapsed between Vicki's abduction and the fall of twilight. He flung open the door and rushed into the main area of the house. A red haze of panic and rage clouded his vision. He almost charged out the front door naked before sanity descended on him. In this condition, he couldn't begin to rescue her.

Rather than waste time unearthing the outfit he'd stashed in the woods, he rummaged through the guest room drawers. As he'd hoped, he found clothes that probably belonged to her brother, including a worn pair of denim shorts and several faded T-shirts. They enabled Stefan to cover himself respectably enough that he could venture onto the front porch without fear of getting arrested.

Still heaving hoarse breaths from his frantic barking in dog shape, he switched on the porch light and dug through Vicki's purse. She carried a pocket address book, with only one "Phil" listed. He recognized the street name, off inner West Street, fifteen minutes across town. Hardly able to restrain himself from dashing in all directions at once, he paused to ponder his options. That barbarian wouldn't hurt her physically, so Stefan knew he could afford a few minutes to plan. Transportation? He could either call a cab, borrow Vicki's car or rush downtown for his rental car.

How would he explain the dog's disappearance this time? He'd left the laundry room door ajar. Let her assume she'd failed to latch it securely. Recalling how he'd escaped from Diana's house, he hurried into the kitchen, opened the window over the sink and pushed out the screen. Vicki would more likely believe she'd absent-mindedly left a window open than that Sirius had unfastened doors and sneaked out of the house on his own.

He glanced down at the shabby outfit he wore. Lacking a white stallion and shining armor, he couldn't show up at Phil's place dressed in her brother's clothes. He had to make Vicki believe he'd found her missing when he'd come to pick her up. He had no choice but to swing by the hotel to dress for dinner and grab his wallet, though he fumed at the delay. Well, at least it was on the direct route to his destination. And he could pick up the car she'd have expected him to drive to her house. On the way out, he grabbed her purse. From what he knew of women, she'd want it with her.

How could she have ever trusted Phil? As a dog, "Sirius" had recognized what a slimeball the man was from scent alone. *If he does hurt her,* Stefan snarled to himself as he jogged toward downtown with Vicki's purse in hand, *the first thing I'll do when I get my powers back is turn him into a frog.*

* * * * *

At Phil's townhouse, in an upscale condo complex in a renovated neighborhood near the historic downtown district, he once again clutched her arm as soon as he unlocked the car's rear door. She punched him in the ribs and yelled, "Let go of me! I'll have you arrested, you stupid jerk." His block looked as deserted as hers had a few minutes earlier. Phil ignored her struggles and dragged her up the walk. She decided to humor him for the moment. After all, once she let him speak his piece, he would recognize the impossibility of changing her mind and let her go. She let him manhandle her into the foyer, where he locked the front door's deadbolt and pocketed the key.

She jerked her arm out of his grip. This time, he readily released her. "What do you think you're doing, holding me prisoner? You expect that to put me in a mood to listen to your spiel?"

"I've read that women secretly like take-charge men. The alpha male archetype."

She folded her arms and glowered at him. "Oh, what pop psychology magazine told you women like arrogant, egoistical jerks with skulls made of granite?"

"Come on, Vicki, isn't it about time you stopped playing these games? Let's have a nice dinner and forget all this nonsense about breaking up." He strolled into the living room. "Make yourself comfortable and let me get you a drink."

She stomped across the cream-colored carpet and planted herself on the edge of the matching couch. There wouldn't be much use trying to talk to him until he played out the scenario he'd plotted. A minute later, he reappeared with two goblets of white wine on a tray. One thing she'd liked about him was his neatness. No wet glasses on polished wood furniture in Phil's house. Now she felt tempted to set her glass directly on the bare coffee table and watch him wince.

"I've ordered us a steak dinner. We can have a nice leisurely conversation and I'll figure out how to make up for whatever you think I've done wrong."

"What?" She set her glass on the tray with a thump. "I don't have time to hang around here. I already have plans for dinner."

He frowned. "A date? How could you do that to me?"

She squelched the ridiculous twinge of guilt his tone inflicted on her. "You have no say in what I do anymore. We're history."

"Not until you hear my side. It takes two to break up."

She gaped at him. "In what universe? Is that your personal rule or what?" She stood up and marched toward the door.

Phil's arm snaked around her shoulders. "Where do you think you're going? I have the key, remember? Just sit down and relax until we're done here."

"We were done the minute you dragged me inside." Shrugging off his arm, she reversed course. "At least let me use the bathroom."

When she headed for the stairs, he blocked her. "Not there. This one." He gestured toward the powder room in the hallway leading to the kitchen.

Of course, the one without a window. She used it anyway, taking a minute to catch her breath and smooth her disheveled hair. *How long does he plan to keep me here, anyway?* She hoped Stefan wouldn't give up on her when he found her house deserted. Good grief, she'd allowed Phil to abduct her. How embarrassing was that?

She strolled back to the living room in what she hoped looked like a relaxed manner. Phil welcomed her with a smug grin when she joined him on the couch. "Okay, what did you want to say? I guess I do owe you the courtesy of listening."

His smile broadened, especially when she sidled close enough for her thigh to brush his. "I knew you'd see reason. Move in with me, the way we planned. We can make a fresh start."

We never planned anything of the kind. You did! Some fresh start, if it meant only fitting her into his template the way he'd intended all along. She forced a weak smile and leaned against him.

He draped an arm around her shoulder, his aftershave stinging her nose. Pretending to hug him, she reached around his front and insinuated her fingers into the pocket where he'd put the key. He went rigid and grabbed her wrist. "Did you think you could get away with that?"

She sighed. "I guess not. My pickpocket skills are rusty but it was worth a try. Just let me go and I won't press charges. You don't even have to drive me home. I'll call a cab."

He clamped both hands onto her shoulders and glared at her. "Charges? What kind of crazy talk is that?"

"Technically, you kidnapped me."

"Right," he said in a "humoring the little woman" tone. "Me Tarzan, you Jane." Turning sideways on the couch, he caged her in his arms and nibbled her ear.

The tickle only annoyed instead of titillating her, in sharp contrast to the way she melted at every touch from Stefan. "Cut that out. It hasn't worked for a long time."

"Don't act this way, honey. We were always good together." Phil planted his mouth on hers. He tasted like mint mouthwash.

Feeling smothered, she turned her face away and shoved at his chest. "Another delusion," she gasped.

"What?" He nuzzled her neck.

"Always good for you. After the first few months, you didn't bother asking how it was for me." Their sexual relationship had settled into a routine that she hadn't dared call a "rut", even in her private thoughts, until she'd worked up the nerve to end it.

She took advantage of his momentary shock to jump to her feet. He seized her before she managed to run halfway across the room. Spinning her around, he squeezed her breast and planted another kiss on her lips.

For the first time, her heart pounded in alarm. *He's actually forcing himself on me!* She squirmed and flailed in his embrace but she couldn't match his strength.

The doorbell rang. He froze. "That must be the delivery guy with dinner. Wait here." He shoved her onto the couch and went over to unlock the bolt. *He still expects me to eat with him? He really is delusional.*

The visitor didn't have a box or a uniform, though.

"Vicki, where are you?" Stefan!

She leaped up. "Right here."

He'd barged into the house as soon as the door opened, before Phil could stop him. "Who the hell are you?" Phil blustered. "Get out before I call the cops."

"Go right ahead. I'll enjoy telling them how you dragged a woman here against her will." He pushed Phil out of the way and stalked into the living room. "Vicki, do you want to leave?"

"Darn right!" She couldn't stop a goofy grin from spreading over her face at the sight of him. Even at a moment like this, the sight of his chocolate-brown eyes made her blood simmer with excitement.

"Then let's go." He held out his hand and she clasped it.

"Now, wait just a minute." Phil blocked the path to the door. "Vicki, you're not going anywhere."

"Sorry, wrong again." The touch of Stefan's hand made her heart flutter in an annoying Pavlovian reflex that seemed to have some connection with those vivid dreams.

"Over my dead body."

Vicki groaned. She'd wasted two years of her life on a man who spouted irresistible straight lines at moments of crisis?

"Sorry I can't arrange that," Stefan said. "This will have to do." He landed a solid punch on Phil's chin, then led Vicki around her prostrate kidnapper and out the door.

To her surprise and annoyance, a fit of trembling overcame her once they reached the sidewalk. She slumped against Stefan. His arms wrapped around her. "Hey, it's all right." He smoothed her hair. "You're okay now."

She leaned on his chest and savored the reassuring drumbeat of his heart. "Sorry to get you into this. I feel pretty silly." His solid warmth reminded her of twining herself around his naked body in the dreams. Blushing, she drew away from him.

"Don't apologize," he said. "Knocking him down was the most fun I've had all week."

She was laughing by the time they got into the car. Her purse sat on the front seat, she noticed, slightly puzzled. "How did you know where I was?"

"When you didn't answer and I saw your bags on the porch, I got worried. The first thing I thought of was the guy you said you'd recently broken up with. So I looked him up in your address book and here I am."

"I didn't think I'd told you his name."

Stefan drove the two blocks to West Street and headed for downtown. "You must have mentioned it in passing sometime. He was the only Phil on the list. Easy to figure out."

"Well, I appreciate your dashing to the rescue. Though I feel like a complete idiot for needing it." Her cheeks grew hot at the thought of Stefan catching her in that ridiculous predicament. Another wave of trembling swept over her. "I can't believe the way he acted. I never thought he'd get violent." She covered her eyes to hide the unexpected tears that welled up.

Stefan pulled over in a gas station parking lot, put one arm around her and guided her head to his shoulder. The gentleness of his embrace left her free to break the contact at any moment. But she didn't want to. The light pressure of his hand on her back made her feel sheltered. "Sorry," she sniffled. "I used to think I loved him."

"Nothing to apologize for. You have a perfect right to be upset." His lips brushed the top of her head, his breath ruffling her hair. "Phil, on the other hand, deserves to be turned into a beetle and stepped on."

The delightful shiver that danced down her spine like caressing fingers shocked her to her senses. Rubbing her eyes, she retreated to her own side of the car.

"You should report him to the police," Stefan said.

The idea sounded great. She started to say so, but before she could get the words out, a floating sensation swept over her. She felt dazed, as if her skull were stuffed with foam. What had she been about to say? Oh, yeah, something about calling the cops.

She shook her head. "What good would that do? He'd say I went with him of my own free will. It would be his word against mine. But I will talk to my brother about getting a court order. I think this qualifies as stalking."

Stefan glanced at her with a wry smile. "Wonderful gift for understatement you have."

"I hope this doesn't cause you any trouble, though. Phil might charge you with assault."

Stefan laughed. "Let him try. Like I said, I'd get a kick out of seeing him charged with abduction."

"There's no telling how judges will react in one of these 'he said, she said' situations. My brother's a lawyer, so I know."

"I still think you should take the initiative and report him first."

Another surge of lightheadedness flowed over her. "No. I just want to forget about this."

After giving her a quizzical look, Stefan shrugged. "Well, don't worry about it for now. Are you still up for dinner? I made a reservation downtown."

"Sure."

He steered into traffic and, a couple of minutes later, drove into the public garage on Main Street. She waited for him to walk around and open her door. He struck her as the type to offer that gesture and he didn't disappoint her.

"I came by your place a little early because I'd hoped to spend a few minutes getting reacquainted with Sirius before we left for dinner. Too bad I didn't get a chance to do that. I heard him barking but I was in too much of a hurry to go find you."

In the upheaval, she'd forgotten all about the dog. "I hope he's okay." But this time he'd have to be, wouldn't he? How could he escape from the closed laundry room? "Never mind. Let's go eat."

Chapter Seven

ꟾ

As they strolled down the sidewalk along the half-mile, brick-paved Main Street in the heart of the historic district, Vicki's hand somehow ended up in Stefan's. His warmth radiated from their entwined fingers up her arm to blossom in the center of her chest, eclipsing the humid heat of the summer night.

He escorted her to a French restaurant where they bypassed the people on the waiting list who were clustered in the doorway. At their table for two, she had to tilt the menu at just the right angle to read it by candlelight but she didn't mind. Fewer visual distractions meant she could luxuriate in the sound of his voice, the aural equivalent of a hot fudge sundae. From the escargot appetizer through salads and entrees, he drew her out to chatter about childhood escapades with her brother and funny incidents on the job at the vet's office. Only when the strawberry and chocolate dessert crêpes arrived did she realize how little he'd said about himself.

"What do you do?" she asked. "Job, I mean." Watching him savor strawberries and vanilla ice cream, she tingled at the memory of what he'd done in her dreams, what she'd love to have that mouth do to her in real life, if only she hadn't vowed to exercise caution.

"Nothing exciting. Freelance website design." He scooped a forkful of strawberries and offered them to her.

With a sigh, she closed her lips around the fork and lingered over the sweetness of the fruit and ice cream. "The work must pay well," she said, thinking of his expensive car. She blushed at the realization of how crass that remark sounded.

He smiled. "Well enough but the most important thing is the freedom to set my own hours and pick my own clients. May I?" He pointed at her chocolate crêpe.

She offered him a bite on her fork, watching his tongue lick off the last drop of syrup and recalling how he'd lapped her nipples in her dream. She crossed her legs to relieve the tickle between them. Hastily shifting her eyes to her nearly empty plate, she took a gulp of ice water to chill the heat in the pit of her stomach. "I'm pretty much done, how about you?"

After he'd paid the check, they sauntered to the garage with his arm lightly encircling her waist. She felt a bit giddy from two glasses of wine and the heat of his touch. By the time they reached the car, she again felt as if her head were floating above her body like a helium balloon. But this time she didn't feel detached from reality. On the contrary, every sense felt sharpened by Stefan's closeness.

When he parked in her driveway, she said, "Why don't you come in and pick up Sirius? I left him shut in the laundry room. He can't possibly have escaped this time."

In the kitchen, she found the laundry room door open. An inarticulate shriek of exasperation burst from her.

"What's wrong?" Did she hear a hint of amusement in Stefan's voice?

Fists clenched at her sides, she whirled to face him. "Look at that! Don't try to convince me that dog can turn a doorknob."

He glanced into the little room, devoid of any signs of life. "Then you must not have closed it as firmly as you thought. If it didn't latch securely, he could have bumped it open."

"Yeah, maybe. Sirius, are you in here? Show yourself or I'll turn you into a rug." No response, of course.

"I doubt he's in the house." Stefan gestured toward the window over the sink. The screen had fallen out.

Vicki shook her head to dislodge the fuzz it felt stuffed with. "I don't remember leaving that window open."

"After what happened with Phil, it's no wonder some details of the evening slipped your mind."

She frowned at him. "Don't talk to me like I'm mentally deficient. Maybe someone, otherwise known as Diana Morrigan, broke in that way and absconded with him."

Stefan shrugged. "Maybe. Except he wouldn't let her take him without a struggle, which I don't see any evidence of. You relax and I'll replace the screen. It probably fell onto the lawn."

"Okay, thanks." Sighing, she collapsed into a chair at the kitchen table. "Do you have any idea where he goes when he escapes?"

"Since he wouldn't go to Diana's place, I can't guess." He exited through the laundry room to the garage and backyard. A minute later, she saw him adjusting the screen in its frame. When he'd finished, he came inside and washed his hands at the sink.

"The only theory I can come up with is that the dog's found somebody in the neighborhood who feeds him dinner." She smoothed sweat-dampened hair back from her forehead, enjoying the cool whisper of the air-conditioning. "But that's the kind of behavior you'd expect from a long-term stray, not a lost pet."

"You have a point but I can't think of any other explanation that fits the facts." Considering it was his dog that kept vanishing, he sounded oddly calm.

"Would you like a drink before you leave?" She wasn't sure why she risked temptation by asking him to linger. When he agreed, she uncorked the wine she'd retrieved from the porch on the way in and carried it into the living room with two glasses. "Since it's been sitting outside all this time, it's not chilled," she said, filling the goblets and setting the bottle on the coffee table.

He sat beside her, his thigh just touching hers and sipped from his glass. "Never mind, we can live dangerously for once."

Letting him get that close endangered her peace of mind, all right. She lowered her eyes and pretended fascination with the flavor of the wine, hoping her blush wasn't too obvious in the glow of the single lamp she'd turned on. "If you could drop over during the day sometime, you might catch Sirius on the premises."

"My schedule makes that hard but I'll try to arrange a time."

"Must be an awfully full schedule." The words came out sharper-edged than she'd intended.

"I have a new client I've had to meet with for long hours the past few days."

"If you want," she said, "I could drive the dog over to your place next time he condescends to show up."

"That's a thought."

The evasive nonanswer puzzled and irritated her. Did he have some reason why he didn't want her to know his address? *What's the big secret? Is he married?* Seemed unlikely, given that not once had a wife or significant other shown up during the cat's illness. *Of course, there's that Morrigan woman. What's the real story behind that relationship?* Vicki wondered whether she'd turned paranoid because of Phil. Or had she learned a valid lesson about being careful with the opposite sex? Trying for a light tone, she said, "What's with this late evening routine of yours? If I didn't know better, I'd think you were a vampire."

"Ah, you have discovered my dark secret. I vant to bite your neck."

The phrase reminded her of the way he'd sampled her "fruit" in her midnight fantasies. A bolt of electricity shot through her. When his hands closed on her shoulders, thumbs caressing her collarbone, she marveled that sparks didn't leap from her skin to his and light up both of them like a pair of Christmas trees.

He nibbled her ear, then her jawline, then the side of her neck. His teeth fastened on the soft flesh, hard enough to tingle but not hurt. She turned sideways and slipped her arms under his to embrace him. His solid bulk reminded her of how she'd felt with his full weight lying atop her on the imaginary beach.

If she reclined on the couch with her legs apart right now, he would lie between them, pressing on all the sensitive spots that begged for attention. She forced herself to resist the impulse. *That would be a very bad idea.*

When his mouth reached hers, though, her lips parted to welcome the thrust of his tongue. No harm in that, surely. He feasted on her and she repaid his ravenous kisses with the same hunger and thirst. He tasted like coffee and wine. Squirming around with one leg tucked under her, she brought her breasts into contact with his chest. With a muffled groan, he tightened the embrace. "Delicious," he muttered into her neck. "Like ripe fruit."

The echo from her dream shocked her into a moment of withdrawal. He couldn't read her mind, could he?

"What's wrong?" He pushed aside the collar of her blouse to kiss her shoulder.

Before Stefan, she'd never suspected that spot was an erogenous zone. So far, his real-life technique lived up to the dreams. *Technique? Is this just a game to him or something deeper?* Vicki shoved the misgivings to the bottom of her mind. "Nothing. It's fine."

She laced her fingers through his hair. He kissed his way back to her mouth and his tongue probed between her lips. Her own darted in response. The hot, wet contact reminded her of how his tongue had pleasured her nipples and clit in the dreams. Immediately, her slit moistened. She crossed her legs to relieve the tingle, thankful he couldn't peek into her mind and see why she needed to do that.

How would his lips feel on her body in the flesh or his cock in her pussy? From the way his hands roamed to her breasts, he might show her any minute now. Her nipples stiffened, teased by his caress through the thin fabric of her blouse and bra.

One hand left that position to unfasten her top button. His mouth wandered from hers to her throat, then the valley between her breasts. A sigh escaped from her, echoed by a wordless murmur of pleasure from him. Another button popped open. His tongue trailed over the upper rim of her bra. Electricity vibrated along her nerves. He opened a third button and insinuated his thumbs under the lace on each side.

Blood suffused the skin under his touch. *If I don't call a halt right now, we won't stop at all. And this isn't a fantasy.* She couldn't fall into bed with him so soon after breaking up with Phil. Aside from their nocturnal imaginary dalliance, she hardly knew Stefan.

She caught his hands and stilled them. "Sorry." The word came out as a gasp. "I shouldn't have let it get this far. I just ended a relationship. I shouldn't even think about doing this."

He pulled back a bit to gaze into her eyes. "You're asking me to stop? To leave?"

She nodded. "I'm not saying forever. But not now." She let go of his hands and stood up.

He got to his feet too and stared at her, his eyes dark with passion. His voice remained steady, though. "If that's what you want."

"Sorry," she said again. "I just don't think rebound sex is a good idea."

"Understood. I'll go. For now." He cupped her chin and brushed a light kiss over her lips. "As for the rest, I can wait."

* * * * *

While driving to the hotel downtown, his cock rigid with frustration, Stefan realized he'd been so worried about Vicki that he'd missed the perfect opportunity to find the amulet. What had gotten into him, rushing off to rescue her instead of searching her bedroom? He didn't think her ex lover would have harmed her if Stefan had shown up ten minutes later. He shook his head in disgust at his own weakness. *She's really getting to me.*

He caught himself worrying about her even now. Why had she acted so spaced-out when he'd suggested reporting the abduction to the police? Was Diana somehow influencing Vicki with magic? The thought stirred protective anger in him.

That reaction had to be a side effect of the same magic that had drawn him to Vicki and made it easy for him to share and shape her dreams, though the rest of his power was still bound. Once he'd broken the curse and regained his normal abilities, his feelings for her would revert to carefree lust. At the hotel, he stripped naked and stretched out on the king-size bed. Only a couple more hours of humanity tonight, a brief window of time to seduce Vicki in her sleep and try again to coax her into revealing where she'd hidden his talisman. Relaxing his muscles one by one and drawing long, deep breaths to invoke sleep, he thanked the Powers that he saw himself as a man in his dreams. Surely that fact proved the animal brain he wore most of each day was in no danger of obliterating his human mind.

Not that the dog's view of the world didn't affect him. When he'd kissed Vicki, he'd felt a sharper pang of need, recalling how much more enticing she'd smelled through canine senses. The flashback had enhanced his arousal and given the whole experience of touching and tasting her an extra dimension. If only she'd yielded to him in the flesh, invited him to her bed. Well, at least he could enjoy her body in fantasy tonight, even if he had to wait for that consummation in waking life.

His cock hardened again at the thought. A dark mist gathered behind his eyelids. He tumbled into the abyss of sleep and willed himself to drift toward the woman whose lush curves haunted him. He emerged from the astral fog to hover above her bed. She lay on her side, the sheet folded down to her waist and outlining the shape of her legs. A satin nightgown clung to her breasts, leaving them half bare and exposing the fragrant valley between them. He slipped into her dreaming mind.

He found her in the grip of panic.

* * * * *

An icy wind whipped Vicki as she ran. She raced through the woods, along the trail where she'd hunted for the dog the night before. This forest looked like a tangled wilderness, though, not the carefully tended suburban park it was in reality. Now the dog materialized but instead of the affection he'd always lavished on her, he raged like a rabid wolf. He chased her with his mouth foaming, eyes glowing crimson. Her legs ached and her breath seared her lungs. With every second, the beast lumbered closer on her heels. A feral growl emanated from him.

She put on a desperate burst of speed. The trail bent at an abrupt angle. She raced around the curve, tripped over a root and crashed into a tree. When she struggled to stand, the dog lunged at her, crouched ready to spring and bared his gleaming fangs. A female voice echoed in the night around her. "You see, this creature is dangerous. Get rid of it. You won't be safe if you keep it another day."

The dog leaped. Vicki screamed and shielded her face with her crossed arms. The animal's teeth clamped onto her forearm. "No! Go away!"

Abruptly the animal vanished. Panting, she clutched the bleeding wound. Another voice spoke. Stefan's. "This is only a dream. Don't be afraid. Sirius would never hurt you."

The laceration, blood and pain disappeared. She opened her eyes and found herself in bed.

Naked, Stefan loomed over her. Even without light, she saw him clearly, as if a cool glow radiated from him.

"You're safe now. I won't let anything hurt you."

Trembling, she hugged herself. "Just a nightmare."

"The nightmare won't come back while I'm here." He sat on the edge of the bed.

"Am I still dreaming?" She scanned him—his luscious lips, his dark eyes glowing with pinpoints of light, the shadow of hair on his chest, his erect cock tantalizingly within reach of her hand.

"Yes. We're both dreaming, just like the other times. May I touch you?"

Her body tingled, her nipples peaking against the snug bodice of the nightgown, heat flowing between her legs. "If it's just a dream, sure." She held out her arms. Just as before, her gown disappeared.

Lying with his chest upon hers, one leg draped over her thighs, he clasped her head in both hands and captured her mouth with his. He drank from her lips as if sipping from a chalice. "I've missed you."

"After less than one night?"

"The timespan doesn't matter. I want to stay near you all the time. Protect you." He scattered featherlight kisses over her lips and cheeks. "Pleasure you."

A mist, redolent of the scent of roses, enveloped them. Sparks glimmered in it, like the dancing lights Stefan had attributed to magic. With a sigh, she wrapped her arms around his neck and returned his kisses. They grew more intense and demanding. He devoured her mouth like a starving man feeding on the fruit he'd compared her to.

By the time his lips wandered to her neck and shoulders, then her breasts, she could only lie with her head thrown back on the pillow as if drugged. His tongue flickered over each nipple and along the centerline of her torso to the triangle of hair below.

She opened her legs wider and he found his ultimate goal. "I want to make you forget all your fears," he said. His breath made her clit tighten and tingle. "Think of nothing but this."

"Can't think," she muttered, her eyes half-closed.

"Then don't." His tongue flicked her clit faster and faster, while his fingers stroked the folds of her slit.

She clutched the edge of the mattress, arched her hips and cried out his name. The convulsion seized her and the throbbing went on and on until she almost passed out for lack of breath.

He seemed to sense when the final pulsations faded away. He pillowed his head on her stomach and ran his hand down the inside of her leg.

"What about you?" she said.

"I'm here to comfort you, not for my own sake."

"Mmm, is that your idea of comfort?" A soft laugh escaped her. "I'll bet you're not exactly comfortable right now." She reached down to give his hair a gentle tug. "Sit up." *And why do I care how a man in a dream feels?* Because it seemed so much like a real encounter, she supposed. She felt a sheen of sweat on him and her own skin felt damp in the cool air of the bedroom.

At her direction, he sat up and placed a pillow behind him. She rested her head on his thigh and extended her tongue to flick the shaft of his cock. It jerked in response. "You like that?"

"Oh, yeah."

She ran her nails along the ridge behind his sac. "So are you comfortable?"

"Hell, no!"

She lapped the rigid column up one side and down the other, pausing to circle the swollen cock head. "How's that? More comfortable now?"

He replied with an inarticulate growl.

She flicked her tongue along his rod while she bounced his sac in her palm. The tiny firefly sparks, she noticed, scintillated everywhere she touched him.

By now his hips pumped, thrusting in the air. “Powers of Chaos, woman! I can’t stand it!”

Taking him into her mouth, she swirled her tongue around his cock head again but retreated when he tried to move.

“Let me,” he gasped. “Got to come. Now.”

She closed her mouth around the tip of his cock and circled it with her tongue. This time, she didn’t resist when he thrust in and out. Her nails skimmed behind his sac and she added the flicker of her tongue to his pounding rhythm. She felt his cock stiffen still harder. A roar of ecstasy burst from him just as he erupted into her mouth.

Swallowing his hot semen, she gently lapped him until his tremors ended.

He slid down beside her and embraced her with one arm, her head resting on his shoulder. His free hand roamed over her cooling body. She drifted into languid calm, his breath and heartbeat vibrating in her ear.

His voice, no longer husky with desire, scattered the pleasant fog. “Vicki, I need my amulet. Is it in this room?”

Irritated, she shrugged off his exploring hand. “If this is my dream, why can’t I stop you from asking me that?”

“This is no joke. I told you, Diana wants the necklace as much as she does the dog. As long as you keep it, you’re in danger from her. The nightmare proves that.”

“You claim she caused that nightmare?”

“Exactly. Give me the necklace and she won’t attack you again.”

She sat up, clutching the sheet to her chest like a shield. “Is that all you really wanted from me? Go away.”

He blinked out of existence. She opened her eyes and realized the shimmering mist that had veiled the room had completely vanished. *So I’m awake now.*

Residual anger at Stefan simmered in her head. She knew it was silly to resent him for a conversation her own mind had generated. Yet this interlude, like all the others, had felt far from imaginary. Moisture still seeped between her legs.

Was her unconscious mind warning her that she couldn't trust him any more than Phil?

* * * * *

On her lunch hour Tuesday, she phoned Nick to ask about getting a restraining order against Phil. To no surprise, her brother heartily endorsed the idea and promised to start the paperwork right away. In fact, he couldn't resist hitting her with a couple of rounds of "I told you so." Though she didn't seriously believe her ex would try anything else after the fiasco of the night before, she felt relief at taking precautions.

When she got home and released Sirius from his new quarters in the laundry room, where she'd imprisoned him after he'd shown up in the yard that morning, he bounced around her, wagging his tail and panting in a goofy doggy grin. "Why did I dream about you attacking me? You're just a big old teddy bear, aren't you?" She ruffled his fur and he rubbed his muzzle on her slacks. "Cut that out. Yuck, dog slime!" While filling his food bowl, she said, "I'm worried sick about the way you keep escaping. Maybe you'd be better off at the animal shelter, after all."

He whimpered as if he understood the threat. "Don't worry—I'm too much of a pushover to follow through. I can't stand the thought of putting you in jail. You wouldn't really hurt me, would you?" He wagged his whole back end, as if to reassure her.

As she walked him to the backyard, the crow swooped from a tree and dive-bombed the dog. He lunged to the end of the leash and reared on his hind legs, barking frantically. Vicki could barely hang onto him and drag him inside. "What's with that bird? It has to be the same one, I think. This neighborhood couldn't be infested with more than one psychotic crow."

Sirius gazed into her eyes and whined as if trying to convey some urgent message.

"Sorry, I wish I could understand you but I skipped my Dr. Doolittle lessons in the vet tech curriculum."

A few minutes later, while she started dinner, the doorbell rang. The dog trotted at her side when she went to answer it. She was surprised to find Phil on the porch. She stared at him through the screen with her arms folded. "You never give up, do you?"

"I just want to apologize for what I did last night. I can't stand to let you go this way. We belong together, Vicki."

The wheedling tone did nothing but irritate her. "No, we don't and I'm already gone." Sitting next to her, Sirius echoed her retort with a low growl.

Phil scowled. "Sure about that? You might not get a better offer. You've almost reached the age where you have a greater percentage chance of getting murdered than married."

"That's your idea of an apology? What I'm getting is a restraining order and if you show up here again, I'll call the cops."

"You're lucky I didn't call them myself when that guy barged into my house and assaulted me yesterday. Who is he, anyway? Your new boyfriend?"

"Just a friend. I'm watching his dog." Sirius punctuated the remark with another snarl.

Phil peered at him through the screen. "Looks vicious. Friend, huh? Hey, is that the real reason you left me? How long have you been seeing that man behind my back?"

The threatening edge in his voice made her heart race. She clenched sweat-slick hands. "You have completely lost touch with reality."

"Then let me in so we can discuss this." He started to open the screen door.

"Don't even think it!" She grabbed the handle to pull the door shut. At the same instant, Sirius charged. His momentum shoved the door open and knocked Phil down.

Phil scrambled to his feet and sprinted down the steps to the middle of the sidewalk. Her head pounding, Vicki grabbed the dog's collar. To her relief, he let her restrain him instead of attacking. He contented himself with barking, fangs bared.

Panting, Phil unhooked his cell phone from his belt. "I'm calling the police. That animal is a menace."

"You sure you want to do that? Do you want me to tell them how you kidnapped me?"

Phil hesitated with a finger hovering over the keypad. "That's a hysterical exaggeration."

"I bet they'll take it seriously. Just like the judge will when I file for that order."

His face reddened. With a belligerent jab of his finger in the air, he yelled, "This isn't over." He stomped to his car, got in and slammed the door.

Without realizing it, Vicki had relaxed her grip on the dog. He seized the opportunity to break free and rush the car, barking furiously as it pulled away. "Sirius, come back here right this minute!"

Instead, he chased the car to the corner, then veered off and headed for the woods.

"Oh, damn, there he goes again." Shaking with the aftermath of the clash, she wiped angry tears from her eyes.

By the time Stefan phoned, shortly after sunset, she'd calmed down. Though she'd been half afraid Phil would come back and start another fight, she'd seen or heard nothing from him. "I'm embarrassed to admit your dog gave me the slip again." She was embarrassed about more than that, self-conscious about talking to Stefan after the past night's erotic dream. Thank goodness he couldn't see her blush over the phone. "Look, when he comes back this time, I think I should take him to the SPCA. He'll be safer there and you can pick him up when you have time."

A note of alarm tinged his reply. "I wish you wouldn't. No matter how careful the staff is, dogs can catch diseases in kennels. As long as he keeps returning to you, I feel better knowing he's under your care."

"I don't like taking that responsibility. Even if he is a great watchdog when he's here."

"What do you mean?"

She gave a brief, understated report of Phil's visit.

"I was afraid that idiot would give you more trouble." The concern in his voice warmed her.

"Nothing to worry about. My brother is going to help me file for a restraining order. Phil has a respectable image to protect. He won't violate a court order and risk getting an arrest record."

"Maybe. Just take care of yourself." Stefan's admonition implied he would enjoy taking care of her. She had to remember that relying too much on a man had landed her in this awkward mess to begin with.

* * * * *

In human form, Stefan lurked under the trees at the far end of Vicki's backyard. He wore only a pair of shorts and a T-shirt, which he could easily strip off at the last moment when he felt the change coming on. Should he risk returning to her as a dog once again? She had caught on to the pattern of disappearances. Sooner or later, she'd work out a foolproof method of confinement. Or she might carry out her threat to deliver him to the animal shelter.

But if I don't hang around, who'll protect her? As if protecting this woman he hardly knew was his job. Yet he couldn't stand the thought of leaving her in danger from either Phil or Diana. *And you do know her, the inconveniently honest part of his mind insisted. You've explored her dreams. Don't lie to yourself, fool.*

And then there was the amulet, the key to breaking the curse and regaining his full power. If only he could get into her bedroom, he knew the traces of his personal magic on the necklace would shine like a beacon to his inner sight.

A squawk drew his eyes to a tree limb above his head. Though he could barely distinguish the outline of a darker shape in the shadows, he had no trouble guessing what creature perched there. "Are you inside that bird, Diana?" he whispered.

A mocking caw answered him. "If you harm Vicki in any way," he said, "I'll make you regret it. You've done something to her magically, haven't you? I'm going to find out what."

After a final squawk, the crow flew away. The now-familiar itching sensation crept over Stefan's skin. Midnight. He peeled off his clothes, stashed them under a bush and sank to all fours on the ground. The change convulsed him.

As soon as he'd shifted completely, he ran to the wall nearest Vicki's bedroom. Through the open second-floor window her delicious scent wafted to him. An acrid undertone tainted it, though. Fear.

Another nightmare. I knew it. Diana's put some kind of spell on her.

He circled the house to the kitchen. Good, Vicki had left that window open too. Luckily, she preferred a natural breeze at night rather than air-conditioning. Careless of her but convenient for him. He leaped up, scraped the screen with his claws and fell back to the ground. No place to grab hold and brace himself. And the way the screen was inserted in the window frame, he'd had no trouble knocking it out from inside but pulling it off from outside would pose more of a problem. Whining involuntarily, he trotted to the patio. He shoved a lawn chair over to the window. Twice it got stuck on the grass and toppled over but with teeth and paws he managed to set it upright. He stood on his hind legs in the chair and scratched at the screen. What his nails lacked in a cat's needle sharpness, they made up in toughness. Within ten minutes, he'd clawed a hole he could worm his head through.

Heedless of the prickles from the torn screen, he wiggled until he'd enlarged the gap enough to admit his shoulders. He scrambled clumsily into the sink, folded his legs under him and jumped onto the floor with a painful thud. A faint moan drifted from upstairs. *Vicki!* He dashed up to her bedroom.

Chapter Eight

ꟗ

Again she ran through a nightmare forest. This time it looked nothing like the placid woods behind her house. Gaunt, gray trees stretched talon-like branches toward the invisible sky. Crimson eyes glittered between their gnarled trunks. A dog howled behind her.

She glanced over her shoulder. Sirius, glowing with sickly green phosphorescence, sprinted after her. Saliva dripped from his bared fangs.

This isn't real. He would never act this way. But her panic wouldn't listen.

Her lungs burned. She struggled to put on a burst of speed. Her legs didn't work. The path underfoot sucked her down like quicksand. The nearest tree limbs writhed like tentacles and lashed around her. Lacerating her skin, they dragged her to the ground, facedown. The dog sprang at her. His weight landed on her back, knocking the air out of her. His moist breath enshrouded her like a dank fog.

A scream escaped her. His jaws clamped onto the nape of her neck. She shrieked again at the pain.

Her eyes snapped open. She lay in her own bed, sheets tangled around her legs, her breathing cut off by the pillow she'd buried her face in. She heard a crash.

She rolled over and sat up. At the same moment, she recognized the noise. The bedroom door had banged against the wall. A dark-blotched shape lumbered into the room.

Sirius! Her head reeled. How had he gotten in? She half expected him to charge her the way he had in her nightmare. She rubbed the back of her neck. No wound, only sweat-dampened hair.

Instead of running toward her, the dog rushed to the dresser. She switched on the nightstand lamp and blinked in the glare. Clasping the sheet to her chest, she wondered what had come over him.

He pawed the middle drawer open and scrabbled in it, scattering T-shirts. "Sirius, no! Stop that!"

He ignored her. After tossing half the clothes in the drawer onto the floor, he sat up with something in his mouth. A small blue object, maybe some kind of figurine. Whining, he glanced at Vicki, then walked to the window.

"What's the matter? Are you trying to tell me something?" Nonsense, dogs didn't transmit coded messages unless they'd been trained. Yet Sirius obviously wanted something from her. He rose on his hind legs and clawed at the screen.

She flung aside the sheet and stood up. Staggering with dizziness, she clutched her stomach. Nausea churned inside her.

Sirius gave her another look and whined as if worried about her. His eyes immediately returned to the window, though and he scratched harder.

"Okay, don't wreck it. I'm coming." Drawing a deep breath, she dragged herself across the room. As soon as she pushed the screen up, the dog stuck his head through the gap and dropped whatever he'd been holding. He sat down and gazed at her as if expressing satisfaction with a job well done.

"Great, glad you're happy." Still fighting the turmoil in her stomach, she closed the screen. "Oh, God, I feel terrible." With her first step toward the bathroom, her head started spinning again.

Standing up, Sirius positioned himself at her side. She leaned most of her weight on his solid bulk and managed to stagger to the bathroom. The dog lay on the threshold watching her throw up, then splash cold water on her face. She let him escort her back to bed, where she collapsed into a dreamless sleep.

When she woke to the weak light of dawn seeping in, he lay next to the bed. Leaping up, he licked her face until she accepted his support for another short excursion. At least her stomach had settled but she felt so drained she could barely stumble from one room to another. Whenever she stood up, vertigo swamped her again. She surrendered to sleep.

Each time she woke, she found the dog on guard next to her. Around noon she peeled off her sodden nightgown and started to dress but immediately realized her muscles would barely obey her. Although she hated the sticky feeling of her unwashed body, she couldn't stand up long enough to take a shower. She called in sick to the vet's office. She couldn't force herself to stay awake more than a few minutes at a stretch, though she did manage to let Sirius in and out a couple of times during the day. She had to brace herself against him and practically crawl from the living room couch to the kitchen door and back again.

When she woke on the couch in the early evening, she heard noises upstairs. She turned on a lamp to discover that the dog had deserted his resting place on the rug. Tentatively pulling herself to her feet, she found the dizziness had worn off. Though her legs wobbled, she made it to the bottom of the steps without mishap. Footsteps paced above her head and a drawer slammed. *Who is that?* Had Phil come back? Or maybe Nick had dropped by. Why would either of them walk through the living room without waking her? And the dog wouldn't let Phil in without a challenge, anyway.

"Sirius? Here, boy." No response. She called up the stairs, "Who's there?"

The footsteps clattered down the hall and descended the steps. The sight of the dark man in T-shirt and running shorts didn't surprise her as much as she thought it should have. She spared a second for gratitude that she hadn't spent the day in a nightgown.

"Stefan? What in the world were you doing up there?"

"I was looking for a thermometer. I thought you had a fever." He put his arm around her waist and steered her toward the couch.

A tremor rippled through her. "Well, I don't. What are you doing in my house in the first place?" And why would he search her bedroom, as the sounds suggested he'd been doing, when the bathroom was the logical place for a thermometer?

"I stopped by, hoping I could pick up Sirius. The door was unlocked." Guiding her to a seat on the couch, he plumped up a pillow to tuck behind her. "When you didn't answer and I heard him barking at the door, I got worried and came in. Here you were, lying on the couch sick."

She felt the explanation didn't ring quite true but she couldn't imagine what ulterior motive he could have. "Where is Sirius? Some watchdog."

"He escaped when I opened the door. I was too worried about you to chase after him. I'm sure he'll be back." Stefan laid his palm on her forehead—a cool, dry touch that made her shiver.

"Like I said, I don't have a fever. It was some kind of twenty-four-hour bug, I guess, but it's gone now." She decided not to mention the nightmare. Probably the virus had caused it. She hauled herself upright and wobbled again.

"Whoa, it doesn't look gone to me. Let me help." He supported her to the downstairs powder room, then back to the sofa. "Are you hungry?"

"Yeah." She pressed a hand to her stomach, suddenly realizing how hollow it felt.

"Stay right here. I'll fix you something."

She leaned back against the cushion and closed her eyes, floating in a haze of hunger-induced lethargy. His caring cocooned her like a well-worn quilt. She reminded herself not to get too used to the sensation.

Shortly he reappeared with a glass of milk, a mug of hot tomato soup and a plate of buttered toast. "I hope this is okay."

"Looks great." Comfort food. Her stomach grumbled.

"The screen in the kitchen is torn, so I closed the window and turned on the air conditioner."

"So that's how Sirius got inside. He stayed right next to me the whole time, until you came in."

"Not surprising. His breed evolved to rescue people buried under six feet of snow."

She picked up the soup mug, gently blew on it and took a sip. Glad Stefan didn't try to make further conversation, she scarfed down the meal in silence.

After clearing away the dishes, he sat next to her and wrapped his fingers around her wrist. "You're not feverish and your pulse doesn't seem fast. Do you have a headache or anything? I could drive you to the doctor if you're feeling not a hundred percent."

A weak laugh escaped her. "For a little bout of the flu? Which I'm practically over already?" As for her pulse, his touch on her skin would probably make it accelerate any second now.

"Are you sure? You look worn out."

"I'm still tired, that's all." She tugged at the hem of her shirt, which stuck to her midriff despite the air-conditioning. "And I need a shower. Ick." Thanks to the soup, now she felt sure she could stay on her feet long enough.

"I'm not leaving while you're still shaky. Come on, I'll help you upstairs."

"Who made you the boss of me?" she mumbled. But she accepted his support as far as the bedroom, where she gathered a fresh gown and robe before barricading herself in the attached bath. She noticed he'd cleaned up the shirts Sirius had flung onto the floor. *So that's what he was doing in the drawer.* Maybe her suspicion was unjustified. "And you don't have to wait in here," she said just before shutting the bathroom door. "I'm not going to fall over and bang my head on the furniture just because you aren't around to catch me."

Laughing, he obediently left the room. It was bad enough having him in the house while she bathed, she thought as she shed her clothes and stepped under the shower spray. If he'd lurked right outside the door, she feared she might have succumbed to temptation. The hot water streaming over her bare flesh and the memory of those shockingly vivid dreams had a dangerous effect on her equilibrium. Massaging her puckered nipples with the washcloth, she wondered how Stefan would react if she emerged swathed only in a towel and called him to join her in bed. She had little doubt he would accept eagerly.

When she reentered the bedroom with her skin tingling from the shower, she wore the robe snugly tied, just in case. He'd followed her instructions, though. From downstairs, the murmur of the television revealed his location. Carefully hanging onto the banister, she walked to the bottom of the stairs. "Stefan? I'm okay now. You can leave."

He turned to gaze at her. The way his eyes raked up and down her body made her legs wobble even more. "Not yet. You go up and rest. I'll stay here a while longer in case you have a relapse."

Since she obviously had no hope of changing his mind, she retreated to the bedroom. As long as he stayed where he was, the stairs and the door between them would barricade her against temptation. She tucked herself into bed and opened the paperback on the nightstand. If she immersed herself deeply enough in the plot, she could forget about the man who'd taken root in her house for the evening. Or for the night? He'd vowed he wouldn't leave until she'd recovered.

If I didn't have plenty of willpower, which of course I do, I'd pretend to be an invalid so he'd stick around. She laughed at herself, tuned out the sounds from the first floor and focused on the novel. It wasn't long before her eyes drooped, her hands went slack and sleep crept over her. A few hours later she woke, hearing what sounded like a baseball game on the downstairs TV. She visited the bathroom and made a bleary-eyed attempt to read another chapter, with the same result.

When her eyes opened again, the bedside light was off. Stefan stood over her.

She sat up. Her drowsiness melted away like mist at sunrise. "What are you doing in here?"

"Checking on you. When I saw you'd fallen asleep with the light on, I decided to turn it off. Sorry I disturbed you." He didn't sound repentant. Sitting on the edge of the bed, his hip not quite touching hers through the covers, he said, "How do you feel now?"

"Fine. In fact, you can leave anytime."

His fingers brushed her hand where it lay on top of the sheet at waist level. "I don't really want to leave. Are you ordering me to?"

Shivering, she whispered, "No."

He leaned over her. His lips brushed her forehead, her cheek and finally her mouth. She parted her lips on a sigh. After today, she couldn't deny that she wanted more than dreams. Would he make love to her as lavishly in the flesh or would the real thing prove a disappointment?

His tongue probed her mouth, coaxing it open. She placed one hand on his shoulder to anchor herself and let the other roam down his chest and creep under the hem of his shirt. After a lingering kiss, he said, "You're sure you aren't sick anymore? You feel hot."

Her cheeks flushed even hotter. "It's not a fever. Not that kind, anyway. And you're hot too." That wasn't an exaggeration. His lips on the curve where her neck and shoulder joined felt like a painless brand.

She trailed her fingers up his chest, playing with the curly hairs. While he nibbled her shoulder at the edge of her nightgown's strap, he turned the covers down to expose her satin-clad body. A breeze from the open window wafted over her, raising goose bumps.

His palms skimmed over her breasts, making the nipples harden instantly. His lips traveled up her neck to her mouth. They tasted each other with delicate nips and licks. The darting of their tongues sent tiny sparks dancing over her skin. *Yep, so far just as good as the dreams.*

Lying on his side propped on one elbow, he swept his free hand down the front of her body and folded the covers out of the way. A delightful shiver coursed over her. He pulled down a strap to bare her right breast. "Last chance. Do you want me to stop?"

With her breath caught in her throat, Vicki shook her head. No matter how reckless that decision might be, she couldn't resist seizing this chance.

He kissed her throat, the hollow between her breasts, then the erect nipple. The moth-light flicker of his tongue made her dizzy. She could only knead his chest while electricity hummed along her nerves. Although she didn't see any lambent sparks like the ones in her dreams, when she closed her eyes those tiny flames ignited behind her eyelids.

Inserting one bent knee between her legs, he pulled down her other strap and licked his way over to the second nipple. She arched her back and rubbed the inside of one thigh against the outside of his. His leg hairs brushed her skin and sent tingles up to her cleft.

She tugged on his T-shirt. He paused to strip it off, then peeled her nightgown over her head and dropped both on the floor. She swirled her hands over his chest and sighed with pleasure as the hair tickled her palms. In the dark room, with only the light cast by a nearby street lamp, she couldn't make out fine details. But she could see well enough to notice how intensely he stared at her face. His eyes didn't glow this time.

Of course not, that only happens in dreams. This is real.

Lacing her fingers behind his head, she drew him to her breast again. He lapped both nipples, moving from one to the other so quickly her head spun. One arm cradled her, while his other hand traveled down her body in gentle, slowly narrowing spirals.

His mouth felt just the same as it had in the dreams. So did his fingers when they finally reached the moist, engorged folds of her pussy. How had she imagined the reality so perfectly? His tongue darted faster, with his fingers matching its speed and rhythm. She lifted her bottom in a silent plea for more. Her hips undulated, straining for the peak just out of her reach.

"Come for me," he murmured. His hot breath made the skin on her breasts prickle. Her nipples ached from the lashing of his tongue. The fingers on her pussy alighted exactly where she needed them, as if he could read her mind.

Waves of pleasure radiated from both spots to merge in the center of her burning core. Her clit started to pulse. Her legs stiffened and locked, while her nails involuntarily dug into his shoulders.

She threw her head back, arched her hips and surrendered to the explosion that shuddered through her.

With her eyes still closed, she felt Stefan move upward, one hand cupping her breast, his leg over hers, his cock pressing against her thigh. "I feel like I've waited forever to watch your face when you come. You're even more beautiful that way than I imagined." When she opened her eyes to find him gazing raptly at her, she almost believed that ridiculous statement.

He kissed her forehead, both eyelids and finally her lips. Returning the kiss, she reached down to grip his shaft. Its fit in her hand was as perfect as she'd dreamed.

When she squeezed it and stroked up and down, the gesture wrenched a groan from him. "Let me in," he whispered, his breath hot on her neck.

"Yes." She wrapped her arms around him. "Wait. Condoms. Nightstand, top drawer."

He gasped and pulled back. "Yeah. Right."

The drawer rattled as he searched through it. A minute later, he lay on top of her again. She sighed with pleasure at the sensations of his weight on her breasts and his cock nudging her pussy.

When he settled between her spread legs, she stared into his eyes. They looked even darker than usual, shadowed with urgent need.

He levered himself up with the head of his cock poised to thrust into her pussy. She raked her nails down his chest and opened wider to lure him in.

Braced above her, he went rigid with apparent shock. "Oh, hell, is that clock right?"

"Huh?" The fog of desire clogged her brain so that she could hardly process his words. "Clock? What about it?"

"Damn, it's almost midnight! I have to go." He pulled away, stood up and scrambled into his shorts.

"Go where?" She sat up. "What in the world are you talking about?"

"Sorry." Grasping her hair with one hand, he planted a crushing kiss on her lips. "I don't want to leave. Last thing I want," he gasped. "But I have to."

She rubbed her mouth, which felt as if he'd scorched it. "Why? You turn into a pumpkin? Or maybe a frog?"

He snatched up his shirt. "Please don't hate me. I'll talk to you tomorrow night." He rushed out of the room.

Still limp in the aftermath of her climax, for a few seconds she could only stare after him until her head stopped reeling. Fuming, she threw on her robe and hurried downstairs, just in time to see the front door slam. *What is the matter with that man?* Well, she certainly wasn't about to make a fool of herself chasing him through the street half naked.

* * * * *

Seething with frustration, Stefan peeled off his clothes and stuffed them in the gym bag behind the fence just in time to avoid getting tangled in them when the transformation hit. His cock still painfully stiff, he dropped onto all fours and gripped the shaft in one hand. A few swift, sharp strokes released the pent-up explosion. Panting, he peeled off the condom and scooped earth and leaves over it. Seconds later, his limbs cramped and fur spread over his body. With a howl such as no natural Saint Bernard ever voiced, he ran into the adjacent woods and raced along the paths until he exhausted his nervous energy.

Worried about Vicki's safety, he returned to her house and scrambled over the fence into the yard, prepared to keep watch until she left for work in the morning. He could catch up on sleep during the day. He didn't dare relax his vigilance while Diana might hatch some new scheme to punish him through Vicki. He hoped he'd neutralized the charm Diana had hidden in the bedroom drawer, source of the nightmares and sickness. How appropriate for her, a fox, symbol of deception, carved from lapis lazuli, a focus stone of dangerous intensity, fitting for a dangerously powerful witch. While Vicki slept, he'd buried it under the bushes, where the layer of earth should negate its magic.

He paced under the bedroom window, more like a caged wolf than a domestic dog. He wished he believed in his deities as more than metaphors, so he could beg them to protect Vicki. If only he had access to his own power, he could raise an intangible shield around her home. He emitted an involuntary snarl. His magic! Once again, he'd missed a chance to recover the necklace. As soon as he'd entered her room, he'd sensed the location of the amulet, in a cedar box on the dresser. A locked box. He'd searched for the key briefly while Vicki slept on the couch and again during her shower, with no luck. If he'd planned the seduction better, he could have coaxed her to tell him where she kept the key or at least left himself time to search further. Wasn't that his whole purpose in seducing her in the first place?

Gods above and below! Is it? Or was it the way his brain short-circuited and his libido shifted into overdrive whenever he saw her? Did he care more about being with Vicki than finding the amulet? Why else would lust cloud his mind so thoroughly that he lost sight of his main goal? He had to regain his magic and his humanity. Once he became fully human again, the compulsion that bound him to her might evaporate too. *Do I want that?* He shook himself as if shaking off raindrops. No use speculating on his hypothetical future reactions. The important thing was to recover his powers. He couldn't live in this ridiculous halfway condition forever.

As for protecting Vicki, he could do that by watching from a distance. He didn't dare return to her as a dog again and risk confinement he couldn't escape. Worst case, she would catch him in the act of transforming. Yet he couldn't abandon her altogether until he'd settled his feud with Diana.

Echoing his thoughts, a crow cawed from a tree at the rear of the yard. Definitely the same crow. He trotted over and growled up at the bird.

In an ear-piercing croak, it said, "That girl means something to you. Delightful. I can't strike at you unless you're weakened somehow but I can hurt her."

Very impressive, Diana. I had no idea you could talk through a possessed creature as well as use its senses.

Obviously perceiving the thought he projected, the crow squawked, "I can do a lot more, as you should know. Give up these stupid evasive tactics. Come to me and take your punishment like a man if you don't want your new girlfriend to suffer."

The sneer in the word "man" forced another growl from him. *I got rid of your little ill-wishing charm.*

"Oh, next I'll do something a lot worse than sending her nightmares. I used this bird to follow her ex-lover home when he dropped in at her office. Later I sent the crow to deposit a focus object on his windowsill and I've been worming my way into his tiny brain. Did you think he'd have the nerve to drag her to his place without a little outside influence? I've planted another idea in his head since then. You won't like the result."

Stefan stretched to his full height, front paws on the tree trunk and growled at the bird. The urge to bark a challenge boiled in his chest but he restrained himself for fear of waking Vicki or a nosy neighbor.

"You have until tomorrow night to surrender yourself and change my mind." The crow spread its wings and flapped into the woods.

If he didn't yield to her demand, he might be putting Vicki's life in danger. If he did obey, he might never become human and would probably never see the woman he loved again.

Love? He sprawled at full length on the grass, his head on his paws and whimpered. Was this anguish love? This fear of seeing her hurt? The determination to sacrifice anything necessary, his humanity or even his magic, to keep her safe?

There has to be a way out of this trap. I have until tomorrow night to find it.

* * * * *

Vicki had trouble concentrating at the clinic the next day. In the late afternoon she went to the courthouse with Nick, where a judge issued a restraining order to keep Phil away from her. She put off Nick's questions about her distracted condition with vague answers. She was thankful to have tomorrow, Friday, off from work, because her brain felt about to shatter like a cold pitcher with hot tea poured into it. She needed a three-day weekend to glue herself back together.

Not having seen the dog that morning, she fretted about whether he'd vanished permanently this time. Had he been run over in traffic or snatched by dognappers? And what about Stefan? When she got home, she immediately checked the phone for messages. Nothing. Although she hated to admit it to herself, she was disappointed to find nothing from Stefan. She still couldn't figure out any reason for his deserting her that way. An urgent appointment? A sudden onset of rampant commitment phobia? He turned into a pumpkin at midnight? No explanation made sense.

To her further disappointment, she didn't find Sirius waiting in the yard. With her pulse racing, she phoned Stefan's home number. The sound of his voice mail came as a relief. She couldn't have spoken to him directly without yelling at him for absconding like an adulterous lover in a bedroom farce. "I haven't seen your dog since last night," she said. "If you found him and took him home, please let me know." She hung up with no further message. She couldn't risk letting the machine record her bewilderment and hurt. She had to cling to some shred of pride.

I was right all along. Rebound sex, bad idea.

She was seated on the front porch with a glass of iced tea, watching the sunset behind the trees, when Phil's car screeched to a stop at the curb. She rushed into the house, grabbed the cordless phone and confronted him through the screen door as he stalked up the sidewalk.

"Go home, Phil. I have a restraining order and if you don't get lost, I'll call the police."

He lifted his right hand, brandishing a pistol.

A cold lump congealed in the pit of her stomach. "What are you planning to do, shoot me?"

He swayed on his feet at the bottom of the porch steps. "Of course not." His voice sounded slurred. Drunk? That wasn't like him. On the other hand, none of his behavior in the past week had run true to form. "I'm going to shoot this stupid thing." He lurched sideways and squeezed the trigger. The giant crab collapsed with a loud hiss.

Her ears rang from the gunshot. The weapon looked bigger than she remembered from the one time Phil had nagged her into visiting a range and firing it. "You still have time to leave before I call 911 and have you arrested."

"You wouldn't." He set one foot on the bottom step.

She switched on the phone and punched the three numbers.

"Give me that, you bitch!" Waving the gun, he lumbered toward her.

Sirius charged around the corner of the house and onto the porch. "Get out of my way, you crazy mutt!" The dog careened into Phil, who tumbled downstairs onto the sidewalk. He raised the pistol and fired again.

Chapter Nine

ꕥ

The dog yelped and crumpled into a heap, blood streaming from his left foreleg.

"Have you gone crazy?" Vicki screamed. She charged out the door and knelt beside the wounded animal, the phone at her ear. "Hello? My ex-boyfriend just threatened me with a gun and shot my dog." She reeled off her name and address.

"Just stay calm, ma'am and someone will be there as quickly as possible," said the female voice on the other end. "What is the shooter doing now?"

When Vicki glanced up, her eyes blurred with tears, she saw Phil sprinting to his car. "He's driving away. But I know where he lives." Sirius' chocolate-brown eyes gazed up at her. She laid the phone on a chair and rushed inside for first-aid supplies.

Willing her hands not to shake, she padded the wound with gauze and tied a towel around it. By now, a siren wailed in the distance, growing louder with every second. She held the dog's head in her lap and ran her hands through the thick, soft ruff of fur on his neck. "Oh, Sirius, I'm so sorry. Please, God, don't let anything happen to him." His tongue flicked out to lick her arm.

A minute later, a police car pulled up to the curb. The officers cut off the siren but left the light revolving on the roof. A youngish man and a middle-aged woman stepped out of the car and strode up to the porch. They offered their names, which skittered through Vicki's mind without leaving a trace, and asked for a report.

Choked with tears, she described Phil's actions, told the police officers about the restraining order and gave them his address and a description of his car. "I have to get my dog to the vet." She didn't want to complicate or delay the process by mentioning that Sirius didn't technically belong to her. "I can't lift him by myself. Please help me."

"Are you sure you can drive, ma'am?" the uniformed woman asked.

"I have to. Please hurry."

The two officers lifted the dog into the back seat of Vicki's car, with a beach towel underneath him to protect the upholstery, while she supported his head. By the time they finished their questions and left, after giving her a card with contact information and a case number, and she got her purse and car keys together, sunset had faded into twilight. Since the clinic where she worked was closed, she would have to drive to the twenty-four hour animal hospital across town. "Hang on for twenty minutes or so, big guy," she whispered. Just as she backed out of the driveway, she heard a deep groan from behind her. She braked and turned to look over her shoulder.

Instead of the dog, a naked man lay on the towel. Stefan.

No, this is not happening! Please, Lord, don't let me be losing my mind. I might need it again soon.

Yet the dog had vanished and the man had appeared. He wore her makeshift bandage on his left forearm, with blood staining the cloth. He hadn't had time, in the few seconds she'd been looking elsewhere, to remove the dog, transfer the bandage and take the animal's place in the car. Even if she hadn't locked the doors, which she had. Besides, what possible motive could he have for such a trick?

"It really happened, didn't it?" she whispered. "Sirius changed into you." Her head buzzed like a nest of wasps and gray spots clustered before her eyes. *Get a grip! He still needs a doctor.*

He started to move, then groaned again through clenched teeth. "Yeah. He's me, I'm him. Wouldn't blame you if you dumped me in the middle of the road." His eyes closed.

She jammed the gearshift into reverse and steered into the street. "Forget that, I'm taking you to the emergency room. And then you're going to explain all this."

"Wait." He spoke so faintly she could hardly hear him. "Clothes."

"Oh, damn, I guess you're right. Stay here."

"Not going anywhere," he muttered.

She hurried into the house, grabbed a pair of her brother's threadbare sweatpants from the guest room, ran back to the car and tossed the garment over the seat to Stefan.

A fifteen-minute drive took them to the medical center near the mall. She dropped Stefan at the ER entrance, then parked the car in the garage and returned to join him in the waiting room. Luckily, it wasn't crowded. She found him slumped in a chair near the check-in desk. "I signed in," he said. "Wish I had my wallet with me. No insurance card." He forced a smile that turned into a grimace.

"I'm not talking to you," she said in a furious whisper. "Not until I get you home where you can come up with an explanation. And don't even think of making up something." She still felt torn between two impulses, to soothe his pain and to strangle him for putting her in this impossible situation.

Again he smiled and winced. "Wouldn't dare. Nothing would sound stranger than the truth."

In a surprisingly short time, a nurse summoned Stefan into an examining room. Vicki tagged along, partly out of concern and partly to make sure they kept their story consistent. Disinfectant stung her nose and, combined with the glare of the overhead lights, made her head ache. She struggled to keep a tight leash on the panic that raged at the back of her mind.

After the nurse recorded Stefan's vital signs, he lay on the table with his eyes closed until a blond, thirty-something man whose name tag read "Dr. Konig" came in. "Bullet wound," he mused after unwrapping the towel and gauze. "The law requires a police report for gunshot wounds."

"We already talked to them," Vicki said. She got the card with the case number out of her purse.

The doctor glanced at the information and nodded. "How did it happen?" he asked.

"My ex-boyfriend shot him in my front yard." Since that statement was perfectly true, she had no trouble looking Dr. Konig in the eye when she said it. She mentally dared him to comment on Stefan's half-naked condition.

He didn't, of course. "Well, you were lucky, Mr. Rigatos. The bullet went all the way through, apparently without hitting the bone. We'll order X-rays to make sure."

After another wait in the lobby, Stefan went back for X-rays, followed by yet another lull until Dr. Konig called them in to hear the results. "No bone damage. I'll write a prescription for pain meds. See your personal physician within a couple of days for follow-up."

With his arm in a sling, Stefan filled out paperwork while Vicki read magazine articles on cholesterol-reducing diets and Florida vacation packages. "I was afraid we'd never get out of that place," he said when they finally headed to the parking garage. A sample dose of painkiller had eased him enough that he could walk and talk without strain. "Getting stuck there until midnight would have been a major disaster."

Fastening her seat belt and starting the car, Vicki said, "Let me guess. At midnight you change back into a dog."

"Yeah," he said from the passenger side.

"And you're human from sunset to twelve. That explains a lot." The panic yammering in the far corner of her brain had settled down a bit.

"I can't thank you enough for taking care of me. Of Sirius, I mean."

"No, you can't." He winced at her harsh tone but she refused to let his pain soften her. "Why did you turn yourself into a dog in the first place?"

"I didn't. Diana put a curse on me."

During their time in the hospital, the sky had clouded up. Raindrops splattered on the windshield when Vicki drove the car out of the garage. Thunder rumbled in the distance, followed by a faint lightning flash. "Why? Lover's quarrel?" She hoped he didn't hear jealousy in that remark.

"We were never lovers."

The hesitation in his voice did nothing to relieve her suspicion. "Then why?"

"I had a casual thing with her daughter. Who's completely of legal age," he hastily added. "Diana didn't approve, so she punished me. Look, you should drop me at my own place. I don't want to put you in any more danger."

"Little late for that. What kind of danger?"

"From Diana. She threatened to hurt you worse if I didn't come back to her."

Her fingers cramped on the steering wheel. "Worse than what?"

"She sent the nightmares and what you thought was the flu. That charm she hid in your bedroom was the focus."

"The blue thing?"

He nodded. "That's why I got rid of it. Buried it."

"Thanks, I guess." Except she wouldn't have become the target of evil magic if she hadn't gotten involved with him in the first place.

"I was going to stay away after tonight. Then your ex-boyfriend showed up with the gun. That wasn't his idea. Diana's magic influenced him."

Squinting at the halos of headlights in the rain, Vicki said, "I can't process all this weird stuff and drive too. Tell me the rest at home."

Over his protests, she drove to her house. There she brewed hot tea with plenty of sugar. Once he'd settled on the couch with a cup, she said, "Okay, give me the straight story. You were going with Diana Morrigan's daughter?" That fact disturbed her more than it should.

"Only for a short time and it ended weeks ago. Diana and I are priest and priestess of our coven. She thought I was taking advantage of my position to seduce Tanith." He sipped the tea and closed his eyes for a second.

"Were you?"

He snorted. "Hardly. She's a grown woman and she was as eager as I was. It was a rebound thing for her. She's already back with the other guy. In fact, she's pregnant by him."

Rebound. Like me. "Coven? Do you worship Satan?"

He laughed and winced. "Don't make funny remarks. It hurts. Those posers? Absolutely not."

"Oh, you're Wiccans?"

"No, I don't go in for threefold consequences and all that 'an it harm none' tripe. That just leads to endless arguments over what 'harm' means. And I don't worship the Earth Goddess. Our coven practices Chaos Magic, which is eclectic and fluid. We each choose our own deities, if any. I prefer to invoke Loki, the trickster. Most practitioners believe a balance of masculine and feminine power works best, so you do get the god and goddess thing often. Our coven has a very simple leadership structure, a priest and priestess with everybody else on an equal level."

"So Diana's into that chaos...whatever...too?" Vicki had no trouble accepting the idea of a pagan coven. Such practices were becoming more common every year, from what she'd read. What she couldn't get her mind around was magic that really worked.

"Her great-grandmother was Wiccan. She was the one who changed the family name to Morrigan, after a Celtic goddess symbolized by the raven."

"That crow! Diana can change herself into a bird?"

"No, that was an ordinary crow. She simply projected herself into its brain so she could see through its eyes and control its body. She cast long-distance spells through it too. That was how she incited Phil to attack you."

Her fear and confusion had slunk into their cage and gone to sleep, at least for the moment. She took a long drink of her tea. The sweet warmth spread through her body and soothed her nerves. "Sounds like she strayed quite a ways from the family religion."

"What we follow isn't a religion. It's a technique of shaping reality in accordance with your own desires and goals. As my old teacher used to say, it's a rainbow of possibilities. I've met people who chant to the Easter Bunny in their fertility rites and invoke the essence of the Sacred Carrot and the Holy Chocolate Egg. Some Chaos magicians are true neopagans and believe their deities really exist. Most of the practitioners I know think the way Diana and I do. We're not hung up on unscrewing the inscrutable and discovering absolute truths. What matters is whatever works for you. We use the gods and goddesses as a metaphor for the energies we channel."

"So you don't believe they literally exist?"

His lips quirked in a half-smile. "Only on alternate days."

"Hold on, you mean there are whole bunches of covens full of people who can work actual magic?"

"No, very few, actually. In our own circle, Diana and I are the only members with more than a vague trace of psychic talent. Tanith has a little more than average but not in a class with her mother. Real magicians are extremely rare. You have to be born with the gift but it has to be trained too."

Right, he'd mentioned a teacher. "Did you go to wizard school?"

"In a castle with moving staircases? Those books give people the strangest ideas. No and I don't fly around on a broom, either. I learned from a mentor I met in college. He was an old ex-hippie and a professor of anthropology. He taught me to channel my inborn power through words, symbols, rituals and magically charged objects."

"That's how Diana changed you into a dog?"

"Basically. She said…let's see…what was it?" He stared at the ceiling as if trying to capture the memory. "Oh, yeah. She accused me of chasing females like a dog. She condemned me to become what I was and stay that way until I learned to care and became truly human."

"I get it. She thought you were acting like a dog, so she made you into one." Vicki couldn't help grinning. From what she'd heard about Stefan's past lifestyle so far, the punishment sounded fair.

He scowled in mock indignation. "Women. Always sticking together."

"While she was at it, why didn't she change you into something really humiliating, like a Chihuahua?"

"Conservation of mass," he said. "I can't weigh any more or less in one form than the other. And she didn't have precise control over what kind of dog I became, anyway. The spell wasn't that specific."

"I don't understand why you're human part of each night."

"That silver necklace you took off me," he said. "The amulet is a talisman, a gift from my old teacher. I use it as a power focus. I channeled my own magic through it and managed to twist her spell just enough that I didn't lose my true form completely or have my thoughts overwhelmed by animal instincts. I constructed a shield against her arcane attacks. The amulet also sent me to you."

"Say what? How?"

"I invoked a need for aid and shelter. The magic fixed on the one person I'd had any kind of intimate contact with over the past few months. You."

She blushed. "What do you mean, intimate? I helped the vet treat your cat."

"Those appointments and the hour we spent together after Caesar died were the most personal interactions I'd had with anybody in years. Far more personal than my fling with Tanith." The tenderness in his voice sent a pang through her.

She refused to feel sympathy for his loneliness or let him melt her brain into mush again. "So that was all you wanted from me, aid and shelter. To think I believed you were really interested in me as a woman. I guess I'll never learn."

"But I was. I am. I've wanted more than that since the first night."

"Speaking of nights, what about those dreams?" Her face burned still hotter but she forced herself to keep her eyes on his.

"Yes, I shared your dreams. Lucid dreaming, not ritual magic. Don't try to claim you didn't enjoy them."

Heat simmered at her core. She ignored it. "That's beside the point. You tricked me—that's what it amounts to." The more she thought about the way he'd invaded her most private self, the more humiliating the memory became. "Every time we met, during all those conversations we had, you remembered every minute of those nights. And you let me believe it only happened inside my head."

"What was I supposed to do, tell you the truth and make you think I was crazy?"

"If you had any ethics, you wouldn't have done it in the first place. You seduced me to find out where I put your amulet, didn't you?"

"That was the original reason. I admit I need the necklace to get my powers back. But it grew into a lot more."

"Don't feed me that line. You were playing me."

He caught her hand in his. "Please believe me, Vicki. It was a lot more than a game or a trick. No other woman has ever had this effect on me. Even now, when I'm wounded." He guided her hand to his lap.

She drew in a sharp breath at the feel of the hard ridge under her palm. Her own body responded with a surge of wetness. "So? That just proves you're male, not sincere."

"I've lied to you, I admit it but I'm not lying now."

She slipped her hand out of his grasp before his warmth could seep into her veins and invade her heart. "I can never be sure if that's true, can I? Not with a man who has magical powers."

"Don't I get a chance to change? After all I've been through in the past week, I realize the mistakes I've made," he said. "I didn't consider the repercussions I was inviting. I should have known better. Our philosophy teaches that choices have consequences. We believe in 'do what thou wilt' as long as you don't violate somebody else's true will. So deception and seduction are okay up to a point but our principles require us to leave a loophole, some point where the target has the chance to make a free decision."

"A loophole is exactly what it sounds like to me. With that outlook, no wonder you can afford that car you drive."

"Hey, I'm into situational ethics but I'm not evil. I've never magically forced a client to hire me. At most, I use magic to induce them to give my work a favorable overview and fair consideration. Same with women. I might use a spell initially to attract her attention or nudge her in the direction I want but that's all."

"You call that ethics?" She didn't know whether to laugh or scream at his idea of fairness.

He insisted, "I never used magic of any kind on you. For one thing, I don't have the capability right now. Diana's curse bound my powers." Once more he reached for her hand but she snatched it away.

"What about those dreams?"

"I told you, it isn't the same thing. And you wouldn't have welcomed me, even in fantasy, if you hadn't desired me on some level."

She couldn't deny that desire. But she didn't want to admit it to him. Not when she never intended to let it snare her again. She turned away from his intent gaze, determined not to weaken under its pressure.

"Hold it." He touched her arm. She shrugged him off. "No, I feel something," he said.

The front door burst open. Diana strode in, rain dripping from her hair.

Vicki sprang up. "Get out of here."

"Of course, as soon as I get what I came for. My pet." She spewed a phrase that grated on Vicki's ears and made her skin and hair prickle as if from static electricity.

Greenish light flared around Stefan. He collapsed to the floor. His clothes and the bandages shredded and fell off. He howled in agony while seizures convulsed him and fur sprouted on his limbs. Seconds later, a Saint Bernard lay in the middle of the rug.

"Don't!" Vicki cried. She knelt beside him and smoothed his bristling pelt. "Change him back."

Diana laughed. "Why? You should be grateful I'm taking him off your hands. Haven't you figured out by now that he can't be trusted? Did he tell you what he did to my daughter?"

"Yes, he told me." Vicki slowly stood up. "Since I found out about the magic, he's been completely honest with me." At least, she hoped so.

The other woman's smile radiated scorn. "Honest? I don't think he knows the meaning of the word. You believe you know him well enough to trust him after one week?"

Could be a valid point. Was she acting like a fool, embracing blind faith in a man who'd given her no cause for it? Not that she would confess her misgivings to Diana. "He got shot trying to protect me."

"Which is why I could break in here and use magic on him. The injury weakened the shield he cast on himself." She got down on one knee and clamped her fingers around the dog's muzzle. "Listen carefully, because after a few months in this shape, you may lose the ability to understand abstract concepts very well. There'll be no interludes in human form to keep your higher brain functions working. You're about to embark on your new life as my pet." Sirius—Stefan—defied her with a weak snarl. "Naughty boy. You'd better learn to behave so I won't decide to make that life too unpleasant. It'll probably be a short one. I'm curious to find out whether you'll have a lifespan of dog years, human years or something in between."

Vicki couldn't suppress a gasp at the image the witch's gloating voice conjured up.

"I'm betting on canine years," Diana said. "Saint Bernards don't live very long. If I'm right, I estimate you don't have more than five or six left."

Helpless anger scorched through Vicki. "You never intended to let him become a man again, did you?"

"I knew he wouldn't fulfill my conditions, not in a thousand years." Diana produced a leash from a pocket of her slacks and snapped it around the dog's neck. "Let's go, Rover."

He didn't move when she tugged on the lead. With a casual wave of a hand, she pronounced a three-syllable word in some obscure language. The dog jerked upright, clambered to his feet and followed her.

Vicki took one pace toward him. Diana spoke again and Vicki crashed into an invisible barrier.

"I don't have anything against you, girl. Don't interfere and you'll never see me again."

At the door, the dog turned his head to cast a mournful glance at Vicki. She watched him led away through a mist of tears.

Chapter Ten

ꙮ

She lay awake most of the night, staring into the darkness and shuffling through the images from the past few hours. Gunshots. Stefan naked and bleeding in the back of her car. Diana's magic flashing like a miniature lightning bolt. Stefan transmuting into a dog on Vicki's living room rug. *Maybe I should say good riddance and forget about him.* Did she even want to remember that Chaos Magic had toppled her world view with a crash? Wouldn't she be happier forgetting a man who'd not only invaded her universe with the incredible, but had manipulated and lied to her? *But he jumped in front of a gun to save me.*

She dragged herself out of bed at dawn, unlocked her jewelry box and took out the silver necklace. Gazing in a fatigue-induced trance at the disk that dangled from the chain looped around her fingers, she decided she couldn't just forget. No matter what Stefan had done, she couldn't let him stay a dog forever if she had any power to help him.

After a shower and coffee, she sifted through the miscellaneous receipts and other debris on her dresser until she found Diana's card. The address, on the Annapolis Neck peninsula, would take less than ten minutes to reach by car. Vicki imagined Stefan, as a dog, running from there along busy roads to intercept her in the parking lot of the vet clinic. *He claimed magic drew us together.* She shook her head. Thinking about the two of them together would get her nowhere. She had to concentrate solely on restoring his amulet to him.

Outside, the wet grass and pavement gleamed in the early morning sun. The overnight rain had cooled off the atmosphere. With a printout from her computer's map program, she had no trouble finding Diana's street. The oversized houses on wooded lots projected an intimidating aura of affluence. Diana Morrigan's home sat directly on the waterfront. Vicki wondered if magic had contributed to paying for the high-six-figure real estate.

When she marched onto the redwood porch and rang the doorbell, a young woman in a loose peasant blouse, with golden-red hair cascading in luxuriant waves over her shoulders, opened the door. Meeting the girl's gray eyes, Vicki swallowed a gasp of dismay. *How could I compete with somebody this gorgeous?* Not that she was interested in competing for Stefan, she reminded herself. Besides, if this was Tanith, she was too young for him. No wonder Diana had thrown a magical fit. *That still doesn't excuse putting a curse on him.*

"Tanith Morrigan?"

The young redhead nodded.

"I need to see your mother. I'm here to get Stefan back."

When Tanith silently stared at her in what looked like shock, Vicki began to doubt herself. Could she have hallucinated what she thought she remembered from the night before? Was this girl about to slam the door in her face?

Instead, Tanith said, "You really shouldn't. Clashing with my mother is too dangerous. If I were you, I'd go home and forget the whole thing."

"So she does have him here. As a dog."

Tanith nodded, still blocking the gap in the doorway. "I can't convince her he's been punished enough but at least I can try to keep anybody else from getting hurt."

"Are you trying to keep me away from Stefan because you still want him?"

Her eyes widened in obviously sincere shock. "You've got to be kidding. I wouldn't take him if you paid me. I just don't want his fate on my conscience, not to mention yours."

"Thanks for the warning but I have to do this." She took the necklace out of her purse and looped the chain around her fingers.

"Okay. I tried, anyhow." Tanith stepped aside.

Vicki stepped into the foyer, with a hardwood floor adorned by an Oriental rug. "Stefan, where are you? Diana?"

"They're in her bedroom," Tanith said. "Upstairs, to the left, end of the hall."

Storming upstairs, Vicki shouted, "Don't even think about trying to keep me away from him."

Diana's voice called back, "I wouldn't begin to. In here."

The huge master suite had a king-size bed and matching furniture at one end and an entertainment center at the other. Diana, in turquoise satin pajamas, lounged in a recliner next to a stereo that played classical music. A cup of coffee sat on an end table beside her. The Saint Bernard lay on the carpet next to the chair. He raised his head and thumped his tail at the sight of Vicki. A tentative thump, though, with drooping ears and a sorrowful look in the liquid brown eyes.

With a smile and a casual wave, Diana said, "Don't tell me you actually want him back?"

"Yes, I do. I was planning to get a dog anyway and I like this one." With the necklace clenched in her hand behind her back, Vicki took a few steps into the room, redolent of coffee aroma and some expensive cologne. Her pulse pounded in her ears. If Diana decided to turn her into a lower life form too, she couldn't do a thing about it.

"Sorry, I intend to keep my pet."

"What if he wants to live with me? Come on, Stefan, let's go."

The dog labored to stand, with one of his forelegs still weak. Diana laughed and gestured at him. He crumpled into his former bear rug position. "You're wasting your breath," she said. "He knows he can't leave. I've laid a compulsion spell on him. He can't step outside the boundaries of my property."

"Really?" Vicki stared at Stefan in horrified pity. He whined and rested his head on his paws.

"Much better than an electric fence, don't you think?" Diana swung her legs over the side of the lounger and sat up. "Better leave while I'm still in a good mood. If you strain my patience, you'll be sorry. Forget about this and I'll forget about you. After all, what can you do? Report me to the cops for kidnapping?"

Vicki moved closer to the dog. Hearing footsteps behind her, she glanced around and saw Tanith coming into the suite.

"This has gone way more than far enough, Mother. You're inflicting vengeance, not justice. Didn't you teach me actions have consequences, even if we don't go by the threefold rule? Transform him back to human and let him go."

Diana stood up, frowning. "Don't you have any self-respect? Why are you pleading for him after what he did to you?"

"I'm an adult. I don't need you to defend my honor. I can manage my own love life, thanks. I'm over Stefan. I've already explained to Rob and it's only a matter of time until he comes around."

"I can't fathom how that man convinced so many empty-headed women to buy his line." Green sparks flashed from Diana's fingers to sizzle around the dog. He yelped softly. "And now he's found another one. Do you think you're special?" she taunted Vicki. "He changes partners with the seasons. If you hadn't been handy to take him in after he escaped from me, he'd never have even noticed you."

That's not true, Vicki thought, remembering how he'd turned to her for comfort after his cat's death. She sidled closer to the dog. She had to get near enough to give him the amulet. What happened next would depend on his magical power. "I'll never know that for sure as long as he's an animal, will I?"

"He's going to be one until he dies," Diana said, "which is exactly what he deserves."

Vicki took the final paces that brought her within reach of the dog. "Stefan, here!" He lifted his head. She bent down, slipped the necklace over his muzzle and worked it past his ears.

"Damn you, get away from him!" Diana cried.

A shower of blue sparks coruscated over the dog's body. The fur dissolved and Stefan lay prone on the floor.

He leaped up, naked except for the silver chain around his neck. "Vicki, get out of here, now! I can handle her. You can't."

"I'm not leaving you."

"Wrong decision." Diana whirled toward Vicki, shouted an unintelligible phrase and pointed with her right hand.

"No!" Stefan yelled. He grabbed Vicki and thrust her behind him. A wave of weakness swept over her. She staggered and gripped the top of the lounge chair. Stefan, though, crumpled to his knees.

"Mother, stop this right now," Tanith said, seizing Diana's arm.

Diana shoved her aside. "I told you I'm going to make sure he stays an animal." Another spell erupted from her. This time Vicki saw a green bolt, bright and sharp as a laser beam in a movie, streak from Diana to Stefan.

When it struck him, Vicki braced herself for the transformation into dog shape. Instead, the beam ricocheted and hit Diana in the chest. The witch doubled over and collapsed to the floor. Her clothes fell away in shreds. Her hands and feet changed to claws, her skin to a tawny pelt. When the convulsions ceased, a cougar lay on her side on the rug.

She raised her head, snarled and struggled to get to her feet. Stefan spoke and gestured. She froze. Her eyes rolled shut and she relaxed into unconsciousness.

Panting, Stefan put his arms around Vicki and rested his chin on the top of her head. "Are you all right?"

Although she was leaning against his side, not his front, she was abruptly all too aware of his enticing nudity. She pulled away. "Of course I am. What about you?"

"Never better. I think that burst of energy healed the bullet wound on top of everything else."

"What on earth just happened?" Vicki asked.

"It's a logical result of the original spell," Tanith said. "Mother imposed the condition that he had to stay a dog until he learned to care about someone else in a fully human way. Obviously he cared enough for you that her transformation spell wouldn't affect him anymore. So it rebounded onto her. I tried to warn her she was going too far."

He cares about me? I broke the spell? Vicki could hardly get her head around that idea. Instead of acknowledging it aloud, she said, "What's going to happen to Diana now?"

Tanith knelt down and stroked the stunned cat. "Stefan, please change her back. I know she probably deserves to go through the same ordeal you did but she is my mother."

He hesitated, his fists clenched. "Oh, hell, all right. After what I've been through, I wouldn't wish that fate on anybody. Even her." He spread the fingers of his right hand, murmured a sentence under his breath and sent a shower of sparks over the cougar.

"What did you do?" Vicki asked.

"Put a binding spell on her. Mercy is one thing. Carelessness is something else. I've made sure she can't attack you or me again."

"I'll keep an eye on her," Tanith said, "and make sure she doesn't come up with any crap about trying to get around that restriction."

Stefan looked dubious. "I haven't noticed her paying much attention to your wishes up to now."

Smiling slyly, Tanith said, "I've got ammunition I haven't used yet. If I threaten to ban her from my wedding or never let her see her grandchildren, she'll pay attention."

He spoke and gestured once again. Diana lay on the floor, naked, glowering at him.

"If it's all the same to you, I won't remove the paralysis spell just yet," he said. "Tanith, do you have anything I can wear?"

She got a pair of sweatpants out of a dresser drawer. "Mother's tall enough that these should fit you well enough to wear home."

He grimaced. "Thanks, I guess. At least they aren't pink." He pulled them on immediately, to Vicki's relief. His unclad body stimulated too many conflicting emotions. "Where's my car?"

"She had it towed." Tanith's voice held wicked amusement. "I didn't think you really deserved to spend the rest of your life as a dog. On the other hand, drop a few hundred bucks bailing your car out of an impound lot? Yeah, that sounds just about right."

After she gave him the information on how to find his vehicle, he cast another spell on Diana. "That's all except the last step in freeing her from the paralysis," he said to Tanith. "You can handle the rest after we've gone. Just speak this word to complete the incantation." He whispered something in her ear.

She nodded. "Hang on, I'll get your keys and wallet and stuff."

"I'm surprised Diana didn't dump them into the bay." After stashing the items in a pocket of the sweatpants, he said to Vicki, "Could you give me a ride home?"

"Sure." She tried her best to match his cool tone. Outside, he gave her directions to a gated townhouse complex on the Eastport side of Spa Creek, just across from downtown Annapolis.

On the way, she brought up a question that had been bothering her since Diana's attack the night before. "Punishing you with a life sentence as a pet seems like a huge overreaction to what you did. Unless Diana had something else against you. Was there anything you forgot to mention?"

"I can't think of any other reason she'd want to hurt me." He didn't sound evasive or defensive.

"Maybe she wanted you for herself. If so, no wonder she went ballistic when you had sex with her daughter instead."

"Not a chance!" After a moment's thought, he said, "She did proposition me once, when we started working together. But it was just a casual suggestion and when I turned her down, she never mentioned it again. She wouldn't hold a grudge for a silly thing like that."

That was her motive, all right, Vicki thought. *Typical male cluelessness.*

She didn't venture any more conversation until they reached Stefan's home. Discovering from one glance at the building that he was as least as affluent as she'd imagined didn't improve her mood.

In the parking lot he turned to her and placed a hand lightly on her knee. "Listen, if you'll only give me a chance, my feelings for you are real. What we shared in your dreams wasn't just a fleeting fantasy."

Ignoring the flutter of her pulse and the trickle of heat at her core, she brushed off his hand. "I can't talk about this now. I need time to think. Maybe I'll wake up and find out this whole weirdness was a dream."

He sighed. "Wait here a minute, at least. I need to give you something." He hurried into his townhouse while she stayed in the driver's seat. Curiosity wouldn't let her leave.

When he reappeared, she rolled down her window rather than getting out or inviting him into the car. With an audible sigh, he asked her to hold out her hand. He dropped an oval stone about the size of a fifty-cent coin into her open palm.

"What's this for?" She skimmed a fingertip over the polished surface—moss green laced with dark brown streaks.

"It's an agate, a gem of protection, magically charged. Just in case your ex comes after you again or Diana tries to worm her way out of that binding spell. Even if you never want to see me again, I need to know you're safe."

She was glad he wheeled around and headed inside without another word, because she didn't want him to see the tears that welled in her eyes.

Chapter Eleven

ഇ

Over the next week, Phil got arrested, had his gun confiscated, bailed himself out and had a date set for his hearing. Now that Diana's poison had presumably cleared out of his brain, Vicki didn't worry that he'd harass her anymore. She was far more preoccupied by thoughts of Stefan. Or, rather, striving to block all thoughts of him out of her head.

She dreamed about him almost every night. Scraps of scenes both terrifying and passionate blew through her sleep like autumn leaves whipped by a gale-force wind. Those images, she could tell, arose from her own muddled unconscious, not visions magically beamed to her in a lucid dreaming state. It didn't help that after each turbulent night, she awoke wet and aching, plagued by memories of their one night of lovemaking in the flesh.

Not love, she reminded herself. *Hot sex.* Yet in more honest moments she couldn't deny she missed him. She'd never felt such a strong connection with any other man. *Maybe it's a leftover side effect from his magic spell that brought him to me when he was a dog.*

She also missed Sirius. For a couple of days she caught herself absentmindedly looking around for the dog, wishing for his shaggy head on her lap while she watched the early evening news. The house sounded too quiet without his panting and the click of his claws on the kitchen floor. She missed the way he hurried to her side whenever she needed protection. *No, that was really Stefan trying to protect me, right?* Her head spun when she tried to sort the tangle of her feelings. She had to remind herself that "Sirius" had, in a sense, never existed. Only Stefan, who'd surely lost interest in her now that he had what he wanted, his freedom and his proper form. She would like to think he hadn't contacted her because he knew she needed time to process the impossible events she'd witnessed. More likely, though, he'd recovered from his lust for her. If only she could say the same about herself.

Each night while reading in bed, she fondled the agate like a worry bead. Several times she almost tossed it but changed her mind at the last second. After all, she might need the magical protection it carried. *No, you just don't want to throw away your last link with Stefan, you pathetic idiot.*

By Sunday night of that impossibly long week, she had to admit the truth. She'd fallen in love with him. Well, she could fight it off like any other fever. After getting over Phil so quickly, she should be able to recover from this virus even faster.

She'd just dropped the agate on the nightstand and reached for the switch to turn off the lamp when the phone rang. *Stefan?* The leap of her heart made her gnash her teeth in exasperation at her own weakness.

Instead, a female voice said, "Ms. Lindstrom? This is Tanith Morrigan. I'm sorry to bother you but I need to tell you something."

"Tanith?" What could she possibly want to speak with Vicki about?

"Stefan's called me three times since last Friday. He's getting downright annoying and besides, I'm afraid Rob—my fiancé—will find out and get paranoid over it."

Vicki scrubbed her fingers through her hair, trying to massage comprehension into her brain. "Stefan? Why is he bugging you and why do I need to know about it?"

"Because he's obsessing about you and I'm the closest thing he has to a friend near your age. He definitely never acted this way over me or any other woman I know of," she added with a wry laugh. "He asks for my advice and then won't pay any attention to it."

"Advice?" *Is there an echo in here?* But Tanith's words puzzled Vicki so much that she could only parrot them.

"Yeah, about getting in touch with you. He wants to see you but he's convinced the magic stuff has permanently scared you away. He's afraid to make the next move."

"And you're telling me this why?"

Tanith sighed. "I'm getting sick of listening to him, so I decided to drop the problem in your lap. Please, put him out of his misery one way or another so he'll leave me alone."

Vicki murmured a distracted goodbye, hung up the phone and picked up the moss green stone. *He's obsessing? That makes two of us.* Would she dare to contact him, though? What if Tanith was mistaken about his motives, if he all he wanted was to reassure himself that Vicki hadn't suffered psychological trauma from her clash with the supernatural? Why subject herself to more potential humiliation?

She turned off the bedside lamp and lay down, clutching the charm to her breast in a tight fist. He'd implied almost anybody could master lucid dreaming. Could she initiate dream encounters too? What could she lose by trying? *Stefan, what do you want from me?* She drifted into sleep.

She floated in an iridescent mist. Stefan's voice spoke from the nothingness. "I feel you reaching out to me. May I come to you?"

His asking for permission must mean she had control. "All right."

Her bedroom snapped into focus. Despite the darkness, she saw him standing beside her, his naked body outlined by a rosy aura. She sat up. "Am I dreaming again?"

"Yes, this is a lucid dream like the other ones."

"Okay but you're not getting into my bed."

He said with a rakish grin, "Then where?"

"How about the woods?"

He held out a hand and she accepted it. His fingers curled around hers. The next instant, they stood on a path in the nature preserve. "Put on some clothes," she said.

Khaki shorts and a polo shirt appeared on his body. She glanced at the nightgown she wore. "Wish I could do that."

"You can. It's your dream too."

When she visualized herself in a sundress and sandals, the gown morphed into that outfit. "Cool."

They strolled along the trail. Moonlight etched trees and undergrowth in a pearly glow unlike anything in waking life. Vicki felt as if she glided over the ground instead of setting one foot in front of the other. Yet Stefan's hand clasping hers felt as warm as living flesh and her pulse raced in response.

"I've tried to stay away from you," he said, "because I didn't think you'd want anything to do with me. I couldn't blame you if you hated me."

"No, I don't hate you." She couldn't bring herself to say she loved him, though. Why invite another kick in the heart? "I understand the predicament you were in. Sort of. It couldn't have been easy existing as a dog."

"It did have its good points. Like getting brushed and petted." He squeezed her hand. "No woman ever paid that much attention to me in my normal shape."

His teasing smile reminded her of the things she'd done and said on the assumption that she was interacting with a mere animal. A blush scorched her. "Hey, wait a minute. You watched me undress."

"Only once. After that, you shut me out of the bedroom, remember?"

Hearing the laughter under the words, she grumbled, "You still took unfair advantage."

"I could hardly tell you the truth. You'd have thought one of us was crazy."

"I did think I'd lost my mind for a second, when you changed in the car."

"You were strong and compassionate. More than I had any right to expect." He cupped her face with his free hand.

His fingers scalded her. She turned her head and his touch migrated to her hair. She tried to defuse the tension with a light remark. "Actually, I still miss the dog."

A flash of green light and the Saint Bernard sat next to her. She stroked his velvety ears. He wagged his tail and panted.

Stefan's voice spoke out of nowhere—"If that's what you want. At least, as your pet I'd be near you all the time, hear your voice, feel your hands on me. How about it? Would you take me on probation that way?"

The sweet silliness of the offer made her shiver and giggle at the same time. "Why would you make a suggestion like that when you have money, magic and any woman you want?"

Once again he stood beside her as a man. "I don't want any woman. Any other woman, I mean. It sounds crazy to me too but you're all I want. For life." He wrapped his arms around her, standing face to face, his thighs and chest firm against hers. Heat radiated from the spot where his cock hardened against her abdomen.

"You told me you cast a spell for aid and shelter. That's what drew us to each other." She couldn't stop her voice from quavering. "How do I know that didn't cause this whole attraction from start to finish?"

He smoothed her hair in a caress that made her wish she could purr. "I couldn't use magic on you while I was a dog. My powers were bound. And I swear I haven't cast any spells on you since then."

"What about you? How do I know you aren't still under some kind of lingering side effect from the original spell?"

"I know when my own emotions are real." The hand cupping the back of her head trembled. "I love you."

The ground dropped away from under her. Her head spinning, she twined her arms around his neck and parted her lips, whether to protest his confession or echo it, she wasn't sure. Instead, his lips captured hers.

He stroked up and down her back, stirring the blood to the surface of her skin, igniting heat deep inside her. Melting, she molded her body to his. While his tongue played between her lips, he clutched her bottom and held her tightly against his erection. "I've missed you," he whispered into her open mouth. "I need you to take me inside you for real, not just in dreams."

"Hey, none of that." She edged away and turned her back to him.

"You told me I couldn't get into your bed this time." His breath tickled her ear. "We're not in bed." He hugged her against him, his cock nudging the cleft of her buttocks.

Liquid trickled between her thighs. She involuntarily rocked her hips to increase the stimulation from behind. Now that she recognized this dream as a shared experience, not a fantasy of her own, she couldn't beg for his pleasuring the way she might have before. His hands skimmed over her breasts and abdomen again and again, each time stopping just short of the point where the blood pulsed, echoing the thunder of her heartbeat in her ears. Sighing, she laid her head back on his shoulder.

"What do you want?" He caressed her in a circular pattern through her skirt.

"You know." Her face flushed with self-consciousness. She clasped his hand and pressed it to her pussy.

He moved away from that spot, eliciting a whimper of disappointment from her. Next moment, though, his hands crept under her skirt and his fingers stretched the elastic of the panties to probe her slit. She tilted her hips to invite deeper entry. One finger slipped inside her pussy. Another strummed her clit. Her breathing and pulse accelerated while waves of pleasure began to ripple through her. Tremors shook her body.

"Yes," he murmured. "Come for me."

With a sharp cry, she surrendered to the cataclysm within her. His hands shifted, one to support her with an embrace across her breasts, the other to thrust two fingers deeper inside, where the inner muscles of her sheath convulsed around them.

"I'll never get enough of feeling you come that way." He kissed the curve where her neck joined her shoulder. Aftershocks lanced through her. "I love you, Vicki."

She had to heave a few shuddering breaths before she could speak. "Say that in real life and maybe I'll believe it."

"When?"

"Now."

Her eyes opened on her darkened bedroom. This time she knew she was awake. Sitting up in bed and turning on the nightstand lamp, she rubbed the gem and wondered if that conversation had sprung from nothing but wishful thinking. *No, it felt too real.* By now she knew the difference between lucid dreaming and the ordinary kind. If nothing else, the burning inside her confirmed what they'd shared.

Ten minutes later, the doorbell rang. Even before she hurried downstairs, she felt the whisper of Stefan's presence in the back of her mind. When she opened the door, he stood on the porch with the silver necklace dangling from his hand.

"Come in," she whispered. She could hardly breathe, her eyes trapped by his intense gaze.

They sank onto the couch together, his arm around her shoulders. Her satin nightgown offered no shield against the heat of his flesh through his lightweight T-shirt. "Here," he said, placing the amulet in her hand and closing her fingers around it.

"What's this for?"

"I want you to have my power focus. Keep it as long as you need to."

She grasped the disk so tightly it dug into her palm. "Don't you need it to work magic?"

He shook his head. "No, I just needed it to break Diana's spell. Now that I'm back to normal, I have my full powers and don't have to depend on material objects. This is my oldest and most treasured talisman, though. I'm offering it as a symbol of good faith. You have to believe I'm not trying to control you in any way."

"I believe you." Still, rather than give the necklace right back to him, she carried it into the adjacent dining room and shut it in a drawer of the china cabinet. Only then did she return to the sofa and snuggle into his embrace. Swallowing her fears, she said, "What you said at the end of the dream. Did I hear right?"

"I love you." He kissed her forehead. "I knew I loved you when the nightmare spell made you sick. It just took me a while to recognize how I felt." His lips roamed over her hair and grazed her earlobe.

Shivering, she hid her face on his chest. "Me too."

"I don't have to be like my father. The kind of life my grandparents had together—now I believe it's not impossible after all. We could have that. If you want it."

He'd taken a bullet for her. Not only that, he'd blocked Diana's spell, even though for all he'd known it would have turned him back into an animal. "I do. I love you. For life."

He nibbled his way along her jawline to her lips. She welcomed him with ravenous eagerness. For endless minutes she drowned in the kiss. When she broke to the surface, gasping for air, she wondered if she would always feel this hunger for him.

Even on our fiftieth anniversary? The thought of anniversaries reminded her she would have to tell Nick she'd fallen in love, as far as he knew, with a complete stranger. "It's going to be interesting explaining you to my brother," she said with a shaky laugh. "I'm not sure how he and his wife will feel about a mixed marriage." *Oh, God, I said the M-word.*

"Mixed how?" Stefan murmured. To her relief, the M-word didn't appear to faze him.

"Religion-wise. I always eat Christmas dinner with them and go to my niece's Nativity pageant at their church. Now I have to tell them I'm engaged to a pagan."

"Like I told you, Chaos Magic is eclectic. It's a system for shaping reality, not a religion. However you celebrate Yuletide is fine with me. Tree, Santa, presents, the whole nine yards. Heck, I could even live with fruitcake."

She nestled against him with a happy sigh. "Sounds nice. I guess it'll even make up for not having a dog anymore."

"Just as I suspected, it's really the dog you like best." His laugh rumbled through her like a miniature earthquake. "We'll get a new one. But preferably not a Saint Bernard."

"Okay. Maybe a nice medium-size Lab."

"And a cat too, if you want. We could have a whole menagerie."

Another dismaying thought popped into her head. "Would you want me to sell this house?"

"Knowing how much you're attached to it? Of course not. I can move in here and keep my condo as a working space. Although you might enjoy staying overnight there sometimes. Ever had sex in a hot tub?"

Her skin flushed with heat as if she'd plunged into steaming water at that moment. "No but I'd love to try it. Only right now we'll have to settle for a bed."

"With the spell broken, we should actually be able to finish this time."

"I'm counting on it. And there's more than one kind of spell, isn't there?" She insinuated her hand under his shirt and laid her open palm over his heart. "Like this kind."

His heart pounding under her hand, he captured her mouth again. When that kiss ended, he muttered against her neck, "Bed. Now."

They walked upstairs with their arms around each other's waists, his hand roaming downward to squeeze her bottom. In the bedroom, he peeled off her gown while she struggled with his shirt and fumbled with the waistband of his shorts. They got stripped in a tangle of cloth and lay on their sides, entwined. His mouth frantically devoured hers while one of his hands raced up and down her side and the other cupped her breast.

"I need to get inside you." While he continued to stroke her breast, his other hand moved to explore between her legs.

She responded with a gush of liquid. "Yes, hurry!" She rolled onto her back and opened her legs. His cock probed her slit.

Instead of plunging in, though, he said, "Not like that." He caught her around the waist and guided her on top of him. "I want to see you this way."

She braced herself above him and descended slowly, taking him inch by inch. When he was sheathed to the hilt, he clenched his teeth and she felt a shudder convulse him. He cupped her breasts and strummed her nipples while gliding in and out of her channel.

Quivering with the effort, she kept the rhythm slow and regular. She could see from the set of his jaw how he struggled against the urge to pound harder and faster. Ripples of sensation racked her. Her engorged clit begged for firmer pressure, more friction. Unable to wait another second, she tilted her hips for the perfect fit and rocked against him.

When her climax made her pussy tighten around his cock, he shouted her name, thrust deep into her and surged to his peak. His climax drove her to a second delirious convulsion.

Trembling, she lowered herself to lie on top of him. With a contented sigh, she rested her head on his shoulder. When her breathing slowed to normal, she said, "You don't have to leave this time, right?"

"Not until you ask me to, which I hope won't be for a long time."

"We'll talk about that tomorrow morning. When you do go, it'll be only temporary if I have any say in it." Her hand wandered over the reassuring solidity of his chest. This time she was sure he was real and wouldn't vanish. "When we wake up, I'll give back your amulet."

"Which will make it doubly magical to me." He clasped her hand to his heart. "And seal the bond between us. Permanently."

Also by Margaret L. Carter

ꟼ

Dragon's Tribute

Ellora's Cavemen: Legendary Tails III (*anthology*)

Heart Diamond

Lion's Bower

New Flame

Night Flight

Sweeter Than Wine

Tall, Dark and Deadly

Tentacles of Love

Transformations (*anthology*)

Virgin Blood

About the Author

ꕥ

Marked for life by reading *Dracula* at the age of twelve, Margaret L. Carter specializes in the literature of fantasy and the supernatural, particularly vampires. She received degrees in English from the College of William and Mary, the University of Hawaii, and the University of California. She is a 2000 Eppie Award winner in horror, and with her husband, retired Navy Captain Leslie Roy Carter, she coauthored a fantasy novel, *Wild Sorceress.*

Margaret welcomes comments from readers. You can find her website and email address on her author bio page at www.ellorascave.com.

Tell Us What You Think

We appreciate hearing reader opinions about our books. You can email us at Comments@ElllorasCave.com.

Why an electronic book?

We live in the Information Age—an exciting time in the history of human civilization, in which technology rules supreme and continues to progress in leaps and bounds every minute of every day. For a multitude of reasons, more and more avid literary fans are opting to purchase e-books instead of paper books. The question from those not yet initiated into the world of electronic reading is simply: *Why?*

1. ***Price.*** An electronic title at Ellora's Cave Publishing and Cerridwen Press runs anywhere from 40% to 75% less than the cover price of the exact same title in paperback format. Why? Basic mathematics and cost. It is less expensive to publish an e-book (no paper and printing, no warehousing and shipping) than it is to publish a paperback, so the savings are passed along to the consumer.
2. ***Space.*** Running out of room in your house for your books? That is one worry you will never have with electronic books. For a low one-time cost, you can purchase a handheld device specifically designed for e-reading. Many e-readers have large, convenient screens for viewing. Better yet, hundreds of titles can be stored within your new library—on a single microchip. There are a variety of e-readers from different manufacturers. You can also read e-books on your PC or laptop computer. (Please note that Ellora's Cave does not endorse any specific brands.

You can check our websites at www.ellorascave.com or www.cerridwenpress.com for information we make available to new consumers.)

3. ***Mobility***. Because your new e-library consists of only a microchip within a small, easily transportable e-reader, your entire cache of books can be taken with you wherever you go.
4. ***Personal Viewing Preferences.*** Are the words you are currently reading too small? Too large? Too... *ANNOYING*? Paperback books cannot be modified according to personal preferences, but e-books can.
5. ***Instant Gratification.*** Is it the middle of the night and all the bookstores near you are closed? Are you tired of waiting days, sometimes weeks, for bookstores to ship the novels you bought? Ellora's Cave Publishing sells instantaneous downloads twenty-four hours a day, seven days a week, every day of the year. Our webstore is never closed. Our e-book delivery system is 100% automated, meaning your order is filled as soon as you pay for it.

Those are a few of the top reasons why electronic books are replacing paperbacks for many avid readers.

As always, Ellora's Cave and Cerridwen Press welcome your questions and comments. We invite you to email us at Comments@ellorascave.com or write to us directly at Ellora's Cave Publishing Inc., 1056 Home Avenue, Akron, OH 44310-3502.

ELLORA'S CAVE
ROMANTICA PUBLISHING